Cathian

The

By Laurann D...

Cathian by Laurann Dohner

Notice - This book was previously published as a short story called 'Captain of Nara's Heart' in an anthology. It has been updated and expanded into novella length.

When Nara Barns and her tiny crew find themselves with a choice between jail or the sex-slave auction block, it's an easy choice. Especially when they plan to escape their buyers as soon as possible, anyway. Even better, Nara's buyer wants her for just six days, long enough to get him through his heat until women from his planet can come to his aid.

Six days and then freedom? Sign her up.

However, Nara's completely unprepared for the impact Captain Cathian Vellar has on her body. To survive his heat, the Tryleskian must feed — and Nara is his favorite meal. Her body can barely withstand the rapture. Soon, her heart is just as engaged. But enduring the pinnacle of Cathian's heat he could kill Nara, and he refuses to risk her life.

The Vorge Crew Series List

Cathian

Cathian by Laurann Dohner

Copyright © July 2018

Editor: Kelli Collins

Cover Art: Dar Albert

ISBN: 978-1-944526-93-1

ALL RIGHTS RESERVED. The unauthorized reproduction or distribution of this copyrighted work is illegal, except for the case of brief quotations in reviews and articles.

Criminal copyright infringement is investigated by the FBI and is punishable by up to 5 years in federal prison and a fine of $250,000.

All characters and events in this book are fictitious. Any resemblance to actual persons living or dead is coincidental.

Chapter One	6
Chapter Two	21
Chapter Three	34
Chapter Four	43
Chapter Five	52
Chapter Six	68
Chapter Seven	83
Chapter Eight	96
Chapter Nine	109
Chapter Ten	121
Epilogue	128

Cathian – The Vorge Crew – Book One

By Laurann Dohner

Chapter One

Nara gripped the cage bars and glared at Derrick. "It's your fault."

The man inside the cage across from hers sported a black eye. "I said I'm sorry."

The words didn't dispel her anger. She wanted to punch her mechanic again. "You were supposed to buy a burner thruster valve. What did you do with the credits instead?"

He glanced away, guilt clearly displayed across his features. "I... Hell, Nara. I hadn't had a woman in months! Have you seen the pleasure workers on the Divian station? I thought the valve would last until after this run, and I'd buy the part with my share of earnings to replace what I'd spent."

Nara's temper increased. "Isn't that ironic. You wasted the money needed to keep our shuttle flying to buy sex, but now *we're* the hookers."

Her navigator, Belinda, sighed from behind her. "Being sold into the pleasure market for a year beats spending five years at Alto Prison. Let's focus on being happy we were given a choice."

Nara spun to glare at her. "*You* might not have a problem spreading your legs for any alien who buys you, but I do. I have standards."

Belinda laughed. "And what would those be? I've been on your ship for over a year and you haven't gotten laid in all that time."

"How about having a choice? To be able to say no?"

"Maybe this'll be good for you. We could be sold to a Yovolian. They're great in bed, have two dicks, and are fond of humans."

"Or we could get sold to some pimp and be forced to sleep with hundreds of aliens. I should have picked prison over this. Why did I listen to you both?" Nara glanced at both of her crew members.

Derrick sighed. "Alto Prison would have been a death sentence. It's a dead moon where they send the worst criminals. They'd eat us alive—and I do mean that. Alto is known for starving prisoners when the food supply ships are delayed for weeks, until they turn into cannibals. It's how they manage population control. At least now we stand a chance of surviving. The bidders in these auctions just want to have sex with us instead of devouring body parts. And bonus, only the rich can afford to lease slaves for a year. They won't spend that much money unless they plan to get use out of us. That means keeping us breathing and healthy."

Nara fought the urge to scream. She was a trader by profession, owned a nice vessel by shuttle standards, and the money was decent. Various types of trade had been prohibited in some solar systems, but the higher pay for those jobs had been too irresistible.

It was supposed to have been an easy run, delivering medical supplies. Her shuttle was fast and hard to detect with the expensive shielding she'd bought. They never would have been caught if the thruster drive hadn't given out, leaving them stranded in space.

"I *am* sorry, Nara." Derrick sounded sincere. "I know we wouldn't be here if I'd just fixed the shuttle. The authorities take confiscated shuttles to an auction yard on Frodder Planet. They're backed up for a good six months. We'll have plenty of time to escape and meet up there. I'll bring the part, we'll fly right out…it'll be simple. You'll get your ship back."

Belinda chuckled. "Look on the bright side. You'll finally break your dry spell and get laid. Maybe you'll enjoy it. I hear the Borters are pretty good in the sack, and they love humans as much as the Yovolians."

"Shut up or I'll hit you too," Nara threatened softly. "You're getting on my last nerve. There is nothing good about this."

Belinda smirked. "Just flirt with someone attractive when the bidders arrive. I hear that's the ticket to not ending up with some ugly-ass alien. You left Earth for an adventure, and here it is."

"I left Earth because there were no jobs and I didn't want to stay there anymore. I could do without the adventure part, and I don't want to be sold to some alien who wants to nail a human just for the novelty of it."

"Human?"

Nara turned at the quiet voice to study a strange-looking alien female standing just feet from her. The woman reminded her of a mouse, with her whiskers and black eyes.

"Yes?" Nara stared at her.

"I heard you talking. Is it true you haven't had sex in a year?"

Nara hesitated. "That's kind of personal to ask a stranger."

"I'm Midgel, and I'd like to make a deal with you."

Belinda inched closer. "What kind of a deal?"

The alien shot Belinda a look. "I'm talking to *her*." She fixed her strange gaze on Nara again. "I'm here to scout a woman for my captain. I believe you are right for him. If you go to my captain's bed willingly for six days, you will be released immediately afterward."

Belinda moved closer. "Why only six days?"

Midgel bared sharp little teeth at Belinda but then seemed to calm down. "He thought he wasn't due to go into heat for another month, but his calculations were wrong. His people are sending females, but they are six days away." She licked her lips, her tongue black and small. "He needs female hormones, and as a human, you're compatible with him. If you haven't had sex with another male in some time, you will scent right to him."

"He's in heat?" That shocked Nara. "What is he?"

Midgel sighed. "You wouldn't know his species. He is rare to this system. He needs your female hormones, and you won't be harmed. But it must be your choice. My captain insists."

She wasn't sure she wanted anyone "taking" her hormones. "No thanks."

"Now hang on," Belinda interjected. "You make it sound as though he's going to take bites out of her, or like she'll be a test subject for some freak with a needle fetish who'll suck stuff from her body. What exactly is involved?"

Midgel frowned. "He won't bite her, and there are no needles." Her gaze fixed on Nara again. "He will arouse you with his mouth on your sex and coax your release from you. That is how he takes your female hormones. Females from his planet consider it extremely pleasurable, and many of them are on their way. His heat hasn't reached the stage where his body is able to," she paused, her features scrunching as she appeared to be thinking, "fuck. He is unable to do so until his hormone ingestion reaches peak levels. He's starving right now."

Belinda shouldered Nara aside. "You're saying he wants to go down on her for six days, can't get his dick up for that long, and just wants to get her off over and over to collect what he needs?"

"Yes." Midgel nodded, pleading with Nara with her gaze. "He needs you. I found no others here compatible. My shipmates will come to buy the female who agrees. It will be six days of your time, you will be perfectly safe. The other female on my captain's ship would kill to be offered what you are, but she isn't compatible."

"I'll do it." Belinda offered. "I'm human too. I'd be honored."

Midgel sniffed. "No. You aren't full human."

A slight blush crept into Belinda's cheeks. "My mom hooked up with a half-Barcalon, but I'm mostly human."

"You aren't compatible. The information I memorized said full human." Midgel addressed Nara. "Please agree. He wishes for a willing female. You will be freed before he is able to enter you, and our captain won't hurt you."

"No thanks." Nara backed away. "I don't want someone feeding on me."

"You'd rather serve a *year*?" Midgel scowled. "Then you are too stupid for my captain."

"They come," whispered a prisoner locked inside a neighboring cage, also waiting to be sold at the sex-slave auction.

More aliens were arriving to bid on the available stock.

Nara's stomach knotted again as she faced the bars.

Belinda stepped to her side, fear on her face, and it only made her worry more. Belinda's tough talk seemed to have been a bluff. "Flirt with the blue guys," she whispered. "They're Avials, a nonviolent race, and their planet is beautiful. Don't look at the red guy. That's a Dolten. They're mean, with a reputation for abusing women."

Nara had spent her life on Earth until buying her shuttle. She'd lived in the human-only section. She'd hired Belinda to be the navigator, but she was also the one who dealt with the clients Nara traded with. Belinda's alien knowledge was vast, and Nara decided she'd flirt with the blue guys if they were the best of the lot.

All the aliens appeared scary, but one resembled a dead ringer for Earth's version of the devil, with his red skin, clawed hands, and bull-thick body, complete with a set of massive, sharp horns on his head. He stopped at a cage down the line and grinned, sharp, bright red teeth peeking from his parted red lips.

Nara shivered with dread, terrified she'd be sold to him.

Her attention returned to the four blue aliens who appeared nearly humanoid body-wise, except for their skin color and braided black hair. They were semi-attractive. She locked gazes with one of them, forcing a smile.

Nara wasn't good with flirting, but she kept eye contact with the blue alien. He paused in front of her. His eyes were black and kind of eerie looking, but he had a nice face when he smiled back. That was encouraging. He stood six feet tall with a slim body. His clothes had to be a uniform, since they were all dressed in the same black outfit.

He turned his head to the auctioneer. "I'll buy her."

The man approached with an electronic device. "All right."

"Wait!" The voice was harsh and frightening.

Nara glanced away from the blue alien—and stared in horror at the devil alien as he stomped closer on hoofed feet, shoving a few bidders out of his way. Panic erupted inside her when she realized he was glaring at her with his evil gaze, and she backed away from the bars.

"I want her," the devil snarled. "I like humans—and she smells fresh."

Fresh? Does he think I'm food? Her gaze frantically jerked to the blue alien, praying he'd offer more money, but he refused to glance at her while he retreated in obvious fear.

"I hear they bleed red," the devil snarled, licking his lips.

It sounded as if he were going to eat her. She didn't want to die.

In a pure panic, Nara caught Midgel's expectant expression. The woman arched her eyebrow in question.

"Deal," Nara whispered. "Have your captain buy me—*please*."

Midgel nodded and stared at someone in the far corner, where Nara couldn't see—until a few aliens moved.

What came forward wasn't exactly an alien, but more of a three-foot-high egg-shaped body on short legs, with a rounded, bald head. Tiny hands waved from a plump chest covered in orange stretchy material. His pasty-white skin also reminded her of an egg. Nara met its round green eyes with dismay.

No way. If that's their captain, I'm not allowing him to touch me. I'll kill him first.

"Twice payment," the egg squealed. "I want the short one with the long yellow hair. Twice payment," it repeated.

Nara's gaze fixed on the blue alien. "Please buy me," she begged. "Pretty please? I'll rock your alien world."

The blue alien peered over Nara's head. "I'll buy the one behind her."

The auctioneer addressed the egg. "Do you want to bid on both of the humans?"

"I just want the shorter one with the yellow hair and curvy body. Twice payment."

"*I* want that human," the devil snarled. He glared at the egg, but the rounded alien didn't budge as he stared up at the male who was ten times bigger.

"Three times payment," the egg squealed.

"Sold!" The auctioneer touched the pad, also nodding to the blue man. "Sold."

A hand gripped Nara's shoulder. She turned her head to see pity on Belinda's features.

"What *is* that thing that bought me?"

Belinda shrugged. "I've never seen one before. I don't even know if it's a male, but I guess it would be. I'm so sorry." Her voice lowered. "At least it looks easy to escape. Hell, just kick it. It'll roll away."

Derrick laughed from the next cell. Nara turned her head, noting the other bidders had wandered off, including Midgel, and met her mechanic's amused stare.

She'd been sold to Humpty Dumpty.

Derrick laughed again. "That puts a whole new spin on balling, huh?"

Nara grabbed the cage bars. "I'm going to strangle you when I escape."

He sobered. "Sorry. It's the stress. I'm afraid that red guy has a horny sister." He lowered his voice. "You'll get to the shuttle first. I'll be there with parts as soon as I can escape once someone buys me."

"Both of you had better wait there for me," Belinda whispered.

Nara glanced at them both. "Rogerville as a backup meeting place, if we have to move the shuttle before it's sold. With our luck, they'll hire someone new or something and clear their backlog. I'm not losing my shuttle."

Both of her crewmates nodded. The station was one they knew well and had visited many times. At least they had a solid plan.

Dread hit Nara when a door across the room opened. Large guards approached to take away the sex slaves who had already been sold. She didn't bother to fight. The guards were hulks of muscles who seemed mean enough to enjoy beating prisoners. Belinda walked behind her for a short while, but then the guard with her turned left.

Nara sent her a worried look, and her crew member winked, as if saying she'd be fine.

Nara was led to a large ship docked to the station. She couldn't get over being sold to a talking egg. She didn't know if she should feel disgusted, insulted, or just horrified. She voted for all three.

More of the egg-looking aliens awaited when the doors slid open to reveal the interior of the ship.

Nara stared at the three identical, blinking white beings—then started to struggle, convinced they'd bought her to be a ship-wide pleasure worker. She hadn't signed up for that.

The two hulks with her gripped her arms tighter, yanking her off her feet. The one on her left addressed the short aliens.

"Can you handle her, sirs? She's a fighter, and bigger than you."

Something moved to the right of the ship's entryway, and then a big animal on two legs, wearing a black outfit, suddenly came into sight.

Nara whimpered. He reminded her of a scary werewolf from old classic movies she'd seen. He had the body shape of a man, tall and buff, but his exposed hands and face were dog-like. The furry hands had claws, and his hairy head featured a short snout, black eyes, and pointed ears.

"He'll handle her if she resists." The egg who'd spoken glared at Nara. "You were bought for our humanoid captain; he should be more pleasing to your tastes. You will find him attractive. There is no need for your fear or your..." He paused. "Insulting thoughts."

Surprise tore through her. *They read minds?*

The egg sighed. "Yes. And we are Pods. I am offended by your term for us. We three are males, and all from the same litter. What you would consider triplets."

"Sorry." Nara remained stunned. She'd never met an alien race who could read thoughts before. It unnerved her just a bit.

The Pod turned his attention to the guards. "She will come with us easier now. Put her down."

The two hulks dropped her none too gently onto her feet and made Nara stumble. The scary wolfman moved forward to grip her arm. She stared at him with fear. *Can he read my mind too?*

"No," the Pod answered in a high-pitched voice. "Only the three of us can do so, but we try to avoid it. We have turned on our abilities to find the right woman for our captain. He needs your immediate attention."

Nara scanned the large vessel as they led her through, taking note it was a first-class ship. She couldn't read the strange language on any of the marked walls, nor did she see anyone as they traveled to another deck on a lift. She half-expected the Pods to roll down the wide corridor, but they walked.

All three of them glared at her when she thought that.

"Sorry. Don't read my mind then." She frowned. "You have to admit, with your shape, it's weird that you're walking." She shot a dirty look at the wolfman. "You can let me go. I won't run."

He growled but didn't release her arm.

She swallowed. *Maybe he can't talk. Maybe he can only—*

"He speaks," one of the Pods stated. "He is mad. He thinks we made the wrong decision, purchasing you for our captain, and we should haul ass to reach the ship carrying Tryleskian women. That's our captain's race.

We have already explained to Dovis that our captain needs a woman *now*. He's suffering too greatly to survive much longer without being fed."

"It is insulting to offer this weakling to our captain," the wolf snarled. "She is too little and ugly."

Nara's mouth dropped opened. "You think I'm ugly? *Me*? You—"

"Don't!" one of the Pods squealed. "He wouldn't find humor in being compared to the Earth version of what you think he resembles. He has a temper. And he'll bite."

Nara sealed her lips together as the lift opened and they led her down a narrower corridor. They stopped in front of a door. The wolfman growled and gave her a rough shove forward. Nara turned to frown at the Pods. One of them moved closer to peer at her.

"Are you familiar with the Tryleskian race? No. You are not. Yes, we are aware it is rude to ask and then answer before we allow you to speak, but our captain is in bad shape. The Tryleskian males go into heat every three years. Our captain miscalculated his cycle. He will go insane without female hormones. We will help you lure him into feeding."

"Thank you," she grit out. "I like to speak for myself," she added, after mentally demanded the guy allow her to carry on a regular conversation. "Lure him? What does that mean?"

Another Pod answered Nara. "Tryleskians are a large warrior race. Our captain is quite aggressive right now, and he'll either want to feed from you or kill you. You need to lure him into feeding to avoid being torn apart." The Pod hesitated. "Yes. I mean that literally. He has been reduced to animal instincts, and being denied a woman for days while in heat only makes him more hostile and dangerous to any woman trying to entice him. You need to strip off your clothes when you go inside. It will allow him to smell your arousal."

Another Pod sighed. "Yes, we are aware you don't want to touch him, and that you aren't a pleasure worker. That is why we selected you. Tryleskian men prefer their women not scenting of other males. You haven't been with a man since your ex-husband stole your money and slept with your friends. You believe all men are assholes. And we are aware that you aren't aroused, but we have a solution." He looked at the wolfman. "Do it."

Distracted by everything the Pods had read in her thoughts, Nara gasped when something sharp jabbed her arm, only spotting the needle when Wolfman removed it. "What was that?"

"It will help prepare your body for feeding Captain Vellar. You would call it an aphrodisiac. Right now, he is in the bath trying to cool his overheated body. He feels as though he is on fire and is starving for female hormones. His mind is confused, and he's filled with rage. You must go in there and remove your clothes quickly, before he leaves his bath to attack whoever stepped into his lair. Your naked body will seduce his senses."

"Put her inside," one of the Pods ordered the wolfman.

"No!" Nara desperately tried to fight.

The wolfman hit the panel by the door to open it. She screamed when he shoved her forward roughly. Nara landed on her butt on thick carpet in a dimly lit room. They firmly sealed the entrance behind her, the Pods and the wolfman still on the other side of the door.

She turned her head frantically, her gaze darting around, and realized she'd entered a large bedroom.

Something growled viciously—a deep, terrifying sound.

Nara sat frozen as she heard water splash. Movement to her right made her heart pound as she slowly turned her head. She knew she was supposed to strip naked to avoid the captain hurting her, but terror hit hard as something large filled the doorway—and she got her first glimpse of him.

"Holy shit," she whispered.

She could only gawk at the extremely intimidating male who filled the bathroom entryway. Water dripped from a thick, shoulder-length mane of hair. It looked golden even while wet, softly flowing with hints of reddish waves. His beautiful cat-shaped, exotic eyes captivated her. They were a soft honey color in the dim interior of the room.

His lips parted, which drew her gaze downward.

He had strong, masculine features. His cheekbones were a bit harsh, his nose a little too wide, and his lips were unusually generous. His teeth were mostly smooth but he had sharp-looking fangs on the top. Another growl rumbled from deep in his throat.

She had to admit, he appeared handsome in a wild sort of way. His face definitely held appeal.

Nara's focus lowered more, noticing how tense his body appeared. He was broad-shouldered, his bulging biceps displayed as his fingers gripped the doorway to the bathroom. There was a lot of golden skin on display too. He had a massive chest, which tapered down to some finely honed abs. She could see every ripple of muscle that led from his lower ribs down to his lean hips.

He was totally naked. And her gaze widened as she took in the sight of one very turned-on alien guy. He looked human in that region, although bigger than her ex-husband had been. She couldn't look away from the thick flesh protruding between his impressively muscular thighs.

Until he moved, taking a step in her direction.

While the wolfman had reminded her of an upright werewolf, the captain had her wondering if some overgrown, steroid-taking Viking human had bred with a lioness. The alien in front of her could have been their mature son.

Her attention flew upward, staring at his face as he growled again, a chilling sound.

Unable to move, too terrified to do anything but stare at him, she heard her breathing increase as her heart pounded, nearly panting with fear.

He released the doorjamb of the bathroom and took another step closer. He snarled again, baring his sharp fangs.

"Easy, big scary lion man. Please don't hurt me." Her voice shook. "Nice Captain."

Chapter Two

The captain's entire body appeared to tighten a second before he crouched a little at the knees…

Then he leapt at her, closing the distance between them in the blink of an eye.

Nara's back hit the floor when his body plowed into her smaller one. He gripped her arms with his hands to pin her flat. She would have screamed if the air hadn't been knocked from her lungs from the impact. The thick carpet saved her from being injured.

The alien sniffed at her, his face hovering over her throat. Nara gasped in air but didn't move, realizing he could tear into her flesh with his fangs. His breath blew hot over her skin with each harsh pant.

He released her arm to grab hold of the front of her shirt.

The captain easily shredded the material, exposing her chest. He lowered his head and brushed his nose between her bared breasts. His wet hair dripped and dragged over her skin when his nose slid lower, toward her ribs. He yanked harder on the shirt, ripping it all the way to her waist.

"Please," Nara begged. "Don't hurt me. Captain? I'm Nara Barns from Earth."

Her shirt ended up completely torn open, allowing him to rub his face on her stomach. He softly growled and released the destroyed shirt. He fisted the waist of her pants next. The cheap prisoner-issue material tore at his slight tug.

"Stop it!" Panic and fear battled for dominance. It might account for the sudden lightheadedness that struck, but her skin tingled, as if tiny little fingers were tapping over every inch of her.

That's when she remembered the wolfman giving her the shot. As seconds passed, Nara noticed other symptoms coming on quickly. She felt feverish and a light sweat had broken out over her body. The feelings scared her.

The captain watched her but didn't do anything else. It gave her the courage to attempt to wiggle away from him. He reached out and put his big hand on her chest, keeping her in place. Nara froze.

He lifted his hand, and this time she tried to sit up.

The captain pushed against her chest again, knocking her flat onto her back. He snagged her pants on one side with a big fist. One mighty jerk not only lifted her ass a few inches from the floor, but completely removed the pants. Her body dropped to the carpet, and he tossed the pants out of sight.

Suddenly, the feel of his nose pressed into the vee of her thighs drew a gasp from Nara. Guessing what he had planned, she grabbed the long strands of mane-like hair. Her fingers threaded through the soft wet tresses and she tugged frantically to drag his mouth away from her pussy.

He growled and ignored her actions, only pressing his face tighter against her thighs.

"No!" He was acting like an animal, so she'd treat him as such. "Bad! Stop it!"

His head jerked up, and pure rage flashed inside his exotic eyes when he glared at her. The snarl that came from his parted lips sounded vicious and threatening.

Nara froze, realizing how stupid that idea had been. He wasn't some rude pet, sniffing at someone's inseam. He was a huge alien who belonged to a warrior race.

One of the Pods had mentioned that, but she'd forgotten until this very second. It was a deadly mistake to make, especially if he decided to kill her.

She carefully and slowly released his hair and pulled her hands back until they rested flat, up near her shoulders. She twisted her wrists and dug her fingers into the thick carpet to refrain from grabbing him again.

He lifted his palm from her chest where he still had her pinned, snarled again as a warning, and continued to glare at her while he grabbed the inside of her thighs with strong hands. She didn't struggle when he spread them wide, too afraid to do so, considering he appeared to want to take a bite out of her with those fangs once again on display. The captain was big enough to do anything he wanted.

"Easy," she whispered. "I'm sorry but you're scaring me. It's rude to just shove your nose down there."

Defiance flashed in his eyes as his hands pushed her thighs even wider apart, holding her totally open, his face just inches above her exposed pussy.

She stared into his beautiful golden gaze, watching as his expression changed to a near-pleading look as he glanced down, a soft whine coming from his throat.

Maybe he can't talk, she thought.

He inhaled, another soft pained sound coming from him, and she remembered he was suffering from a need of female hormones. That mousy alien had warned her what would be in store for her if she'd agreed.

Nara swallowed hard. He could force her—hurt her, for that matter, do anything he wanted. Instead, he hesitated, hovering just inches from taking what he needed. He waited until she reluctantly nodded.

A deal was a deal. At least he wasn't that horned devil guy who'd talked about her like she were food or a torture candidate.

"Okay. I'm still scared, but strangely starting to get turned on. Your people drugged me with something and it's definitely taking effect." She drew in a deep breath. "Just don't hurt me."

His gaze lowered to her pussy. A soft rumble came from his parted lips. It wasn't a frightening sound this time. His nostrils flared when he sniffed at her again, and then he lowered his face.

Nara tensed as he nudged her labia. It surprised her when he slowly nuzzled against her, spreading her slightly with his nose, sniffing more. She clawed the carpet, forcing herself to stay still even though the urge to twist away grew strong.

She never could have expected how it would feel when his tongue darted out and glided through her slit.

Then he hit her clit, and she gasped. It didn't hurt at all, but the instant jolt of lust felt as foreign as he was.

He shifted his hold on her thighs, until his thumbs spread her sex wide open to his mouth. He had a thick tongue, wet and hot. He licked her in long, slow strokes. Feeling overwhelmed, she tried to wiggle away but he held her firm, his upper body pressing against her to drive her ass firmly down into the carpet.

"Wait," she gasped.

He ignored her, moving back up from her slit to her clit. He paused, and then began licking her again.

Nara threw her head back, her fingers clawing the carpet as sensations swamped her, strong as electric volts. Pleasure spread through her lower body up to her stomach, making it tighten, and to her chest, where her nipples hardened.

"Bad," she moaned. "*Really* bad."

He growled against her clit before his tongue moved away. She felt air blow across the bundle of nerves, making her keenly aware of the ache either he or the drugs had created, a second before he pressed his tongue against her entrance, pushing inside her pussy. He pierced her with it, and growled louder. The sound created vibrations that heightened her pleasure even more.

She was stunned again when he shook his head a little, pressing his face tighter between her spread thighs to push his tongue deeper. She felt it moving languidly, as though he were kissing her. The feeling was strange, but *so* good. She'd never had a man do that before. She tried to ease away from his mouth again, for a moment of relief, but his hands held her pinned flat and open.

He withdrew his tongue, a darker snarl coming from him as he found her clit again. He didn't slowly lick this time. He lapped with sure, fast strokes, almost frantically, with just the tip of his tongue.

Pleasure tore through Nara, raw sensations she couldn't escape from, what with his strong hold on her and his tongue moving ruthlessly. She tensed, her body going rigid as she panted, moans tearing through her parted lips that she couldn't hold back. Her vaginal walls clenched, tightened, and she knew she was going to come. It surprised her, but it felt so good she got over the shock quickly as she cried out, ecstasy rolling through her.

"Oh God!" she shouted.

He snarled something, perhaps a word she didn't understand, before he stopped touching her clit to enter her pussy with his tongue again, shoving it inside deep, lapping at her release.

Now she understood what feeding him meant.

The sensation of that tongue extended her climax until she nearly passed out from oversensitivity. He withdrew it, and her body slumped to the carpet. The sound of her heavy breathing seemed loud inside the room, and she forced her eyes open to stare at the dim ceiling above.

He'd licked her until she'd climaxed. It sure hadn't hurt. The drugs she'd been given made her feel a little sleepy at that moment, but she fought the urge to pass out. She lifted her head to stare at the man still holding her thighs spread wide.

His golden gaze studied her back.

He moved, releasing her legs, and his body rose from the floor. Nara tensed as the massive alien crawled up her body until his face hovered over her breasts. He flattened his palms on the carpet next to her ribs, caging her under him, and his hips kept her thighs spread. He searched her gaze, seeming to look for something.

"Cathian." He had a deep, husky voice when he spoke.

"What?"

"My name is Cathian."

"But your crew called you Vellar."

He slowly lowered his upper chest until their skin was plastered together. His body felt unusually warm, but he didn't crush her under his massive frame, bracing just enough weight with his forearms to avoid that.

"My official title is Captain Cathian Vellar, Ambassador to Tryleskian. You will call me Cathian." He paused. "What is your name?"

She'd already told him but he'd seemed a little irate at the time. "Nara Barns. I'm a captain too. At least, I was until I was arrested for illegal trade and the authorities impounded my shuttle."

A frown twisted his lips. "You're a sex slave. I was told they planned to buy one to feed me."

She wanted to wince over him believing she was a hooker. "I'm a trader by profession, but I got caught in the wrong solar system."

"Hm." His gaze lowered to her throat then flicked to her blonde hair spread out next to her head. "Illegal drugs?"

"Medicine only. I'm not a pusher of entertainment crap."

He studied her eyes. "I don't care as long as you don't take them. And you don't."

"How do you know?"

"I'd taste them on you and smell them. I'm a Tryleskian."

"I don't know what that means. I've never heard of your people before today."

He sniffed. "They did give you Assionex."

"What's that?"

"The drug females take to help stimulate and prepare them before males go into heat."

"That wolfman gave me a shot without my permission."

Humor curved his lips. "You mean Dovis. He's my best friend and first officer, in charge of my ship when I'm not. I know what a wolf is, and he'd be offended to be compared to a dog. Never call him that to his face. Did they tell you what I'm going to do to you?"

"Sort of."

His beautiful eyes narrowed until his thick eyelashes nearly obscured his golden irises. "I'll be senseless again soon, but right after I ingest your hormones I will have minutes of lucidity. You produce strong amounts, or I'd still be consuming you. I'm glad that theory about your race has proven true."

"What theory?"

"Human females have strong sexual hormones in their fluids."

That news surprised her. "We do?"

A soft growl made his chest vibrate against hers. "Yes. And I'm starving. I need you again."

"But we just—"

He pushed up, his chest sliding across her stomach as he lowered himself down her body. "Don't fight me. I become violent, in case they didn't warn you. Females from my planet are traveling to meet us. They will arrive in time for me to pick one of them with whom to complete the heat cycle. You're lucky for that."

Nara didn't fight as he spread her thighs wider when he stretched out on his belly, his face inches from her pussy again. One of his hands adjusted her until his mouth and her clit lined up. She still didn't protest, the current conversation distracting her.

"Why am I lucky?"

Their gazes met and held. "I'll have ingested enough hormones from feeding off you to need to release my seed at the end of my heat cycle." He darted a glance at her pussy then looked at her again. "You're small, and I'm afraid you couldn't take the rough mating that will result during my release."

"What does that mean?"

His fingers spread her labia open, exposing her to him again. "It means after feeding on your hormones, I'll be ready to spill my seed for hours to complete the cycle when I've had my fill. You don't want to know what that entails."

She swallowed down a little fear. "What if that ship doesn't reach us before you, um, need to do that? I want to know."

He tilted his head, watching her. "My crew will do what needs done. You will be secured face down and bent forward for easier penetration, and I'll take you for hours, unable to stop until all the hormones are released with my seed. It is a bit barbaric, but the females from my planet enjoy it, from what they've assured me. I'm not certain it would have the same effect on a human. But I'm afraid with your smaller, weaker form, I'd harm you." He growled. "Hungry…"

Nara's mouth opened to ask him the dozens of questions that filled her mind, but he buried his face, his tongue aiming straight for her clit.

Pleasure gripped her and moans tore from her parted lips instead. The drug obviously helped her recover faster, and she ached for release almost the second he started. She shifted her legs and rested her heels on his shoulders. He didn't seem to care that her thighs pillowed each side of his face in that position.

She came a second time. Cathian pulled her thighs apart and drove his tongue inside her pussy, fucking her with it. She didn't mean to move, but her hips rocked hard against his tongue. The sensation made her ache for more.

He pinned her again until she couldn't move from the waist down. When he was done, he used his forearms to brace his weight, climbing higher up her body until he collapsed over her, his head between her breasts and his chest against her stomach.

Nara caught her breath and looked down. She realized his eyes were closed—and then he started to lightly snore.

Stunned, she just gaped at him. *He might be an alien but he's still a male, passing out after getting what he wants from me.* She resisted the snort that nearly surfaced at that thought. Her body actually ached for more after being tongue screwed enough that she was turned-on all over again, and her clit throbbed uncomfortably as she lay there.

She hoped the drugs were the cause.

She wiggled around in an attempt to shift his heavy body off hers, wanting to get out from under him. He growled in his sleep, a mean sound, and his legs shifted to the outside of her thighs, pinning her down more firmly. He continued to lightly snore when she ceased her movements.

Breathing became tough as he relaxed further in his slumber, crushing her into the thick carpet. He had to weigh well over two hundred and fifty pounds. Nara hesitated and then touched his hair. The soft, thick texture curled slightly around her shaking fingers. Next, she touched his broad shoulders, trying to push him to one side and move him enough to wiggle out from under his dead weight.

He growled again and his arms and legs tightened around her body, clinging.

He wasn't going to let her go in his sleep. Nara took a shallow breath, guessing it was some weird alien instinct to keep her close. She closed her eyes, concentrated, and thought of the three Pod guys. Could they hear her thoughts still?

Help! Can you hear me? Can you still read my mind? Your captain is on top of me, passed out, and I can't move him. Please send that wolfman in here to lift him off.

Minutes passed without the door opening to the private cabin. Frustration and irritation battled inside Nara. She softly cursed, trying again to find the strength in her arms to push the captain's shoulders up. If she could just move him a few inches, she might be able to twist her upper body enough to make him slide off her. Obviously, the Pod guys were either not listening to her thoughts or they were ignoring her plea for help. She assumed the latter. They had tossed her into Cathian's cabin, after all, regardless of her safety.

Her arms strained, but she couldn't lift him. Tryleskian alien men were *huge*. She wiggled her ass, trying to at least separate them that way—but halted that action when hot, thick flesh pressed against her thigh.

Cathian might be passed out, but part of him was still awake and hard.

She tried to move the other way, but that didn't work either. If anything, his cock seemed to press more firmly against her thigh. She froze, realizing she wasn't imagining it. His cock had definitely grown stiffer.

A soft growl came from his lips and his body tensed.

Nara looked down to stare at his face and watched his eyes open slowly. He stared back, their gazes meeting.

"Please get off me."

He moved his hips, pressing his erection harder against her inner thigh.

Alarm tore through her. She shook her head. "You said you couldn't have sex until you had all the hormones you needed."

His mouth opened and his tongue slid out, wetting his lower lip. Passion flared in his eyes as he braced his arms, lifted off her a little, until some of his weight eased from her. She adjusted her arms to push herself up but he lowered his body again.

"I can have sex, but I can't find release until all the hormones I need trigger that part of my heat." He rubbed against her thigh, moaning. "It is still pleasurable."

"I didn't sign up for that. I was told no penetration, just oral, and you already broke that promise with your tongue."

He growled, a flash of irritation on his handsome features. "It's how I feed." He eased down her body, shoving at her thighs. "I'm hungry again."

"No way. You just—"

A snarl tore from him before he buried his face, spreading her open for his tongue, and started to lap at her clit again.

Nara moaned. She was in a world of trouble if this was an indication of the next six days. He'd kill her. No one could survive climaxing over and over for days. He hadn't even slept for more than fifteen minutes.

It took longer, but she came, and Nara knew what would happen next. He entered her pussy with his tongue, lapping up her release, growling softly all the while. When he'd had enough, he rose up and collapsed on top of her again, pinning her under his massive body.

The snoring didn't bother her this time, She yawned, exhausted from the stress of being a prisoner, of being sold at auction, and the multiple orgasms.

Chapter Three

Nara woke when a pair of strong arms slid between her and the carpet. She opened her eyes as Cathian stood, holding her against his chest. He turned, walked to the big bed, and gently eased her down.

He backed away, strode across the room to the door, and bent forward. It gave her an excellent view of his muscular ass. He had a nice one. He turned holding a tray and approached the bed.

"They delivered food."

She sat up, feeling self-conscious since she was naked. He didn't seem to have a problem with being in that state, as he sat on the bed a few feet away, placing the tray between them. She stared at the two plates and cups on the blue surface. It looked as if they were being served a form of thick meat jerky bars.

"What are they?"

He picked one up off a plate and lifted it to her mouth. "Open."

It had to beat the slop they'd served her at the auction house. It had been like watery oatmeal that tasted moldy. She parted her lips and he pushed the tip inside.

"Bite. They're soft. Your teeth should work."

She bit down and discovered he was right. She chewed, the flavor of beef and maybe broccoli bursting across her taste buds. He took a much larger bite than she had, watching her closely.

She swallowed. "That's pretty tasty."

He motioned with his free hand for her to eat. She didn't hesitate to take a bar and bite into it. He got about three bites from each one, while she took six. Two bars later, she felt full. Cathian ate all the ones on his plate and frowned at her leftovers.

"I'm good. Eat them if you can."

He polished off her remaining two bars and sipped from his cup. She decided to test the drink. It wasn't bad either, reminding her of very weak black tea.

He downed his drink and stood, entering the bathroom and leaving her alone in the bedroom. She glanced around his cabin. It was three times the size of the one she lived in on her shuttle.

The bathroom door opened moments later and Cathian walked right over to her, took the cup from her hand, and replaced it on the tray. He returned it to the floor near the door before facing her.

"Use the bathroom. My hunger for food has been appeased. I need you."

She felt a blush heat her cheeks, not needing him to spell out what he meant. She rose and hurried into the bathroom, closing the door behind her. The bathroom was way nicer and larger than hers too. He had a shower, and a huge tub that reminded her of a four-person Jacuzzi on Earth.

The door opened behind her and she startled, spinning around. Cathian strode in as if he had every right—which he did, since they were his cabin. "Shower. I laid out a towel and a toothbrush for you. Don't delay." His voice deepened. "I *need* you."

She got it. "Are you going to stay in here?"

He growled, anger flashing in his eyes, but he left. The door slammed, his message clear. He didn't like to be kept waiting.

She quickly stepped into the shower. Water automatically came on. It was hot but not overly so. She closed her eyes for a few seconds, just enjoying the feel of water sluicing down her body. Even over the shower, she heard a loud snarl.

Nara made a low growl of her own before she opened her eyes, reaching for hair cleaner. It had to be the fastest she'd ever attended to her body. She got out, wrapped the towel around her middle, and brushed her teeth. Right as she rinsed her mouth and bent over to spit, two big arms wrapped around her body.

She gasped, dropping the toothbrush as Cathian hauled her off her feet. He carried her in front of his body to the edge of the bed, set her on her feet, and ripped the towel off. He pushed her lightly and she landed face down on the bed. He gripped her ankles, forcing her to roll onto her back. Then the big guy let her go, hooked her knees, and jerked them up and apart.

Before she could even recover from being manhandled, he had his face pressed against her pussy. His mouth latched onto her clit, licking and sucking.

"Fuck," she moaned, clawing the bedding.

His mattress was a lot softer than the carpet had been. She adjusted her legs, placing her feet on his back. He slid his hands up to her ass, cupping each cheek to hold her in place against his mouth. She threw her head back, closing her eyes. Pleasure tore through her, building until every muscle in her body tensed, and then the climax had her calling out his name.

He eased off her clit, released her ass with his big hands, and gripped her thighs. He shoved them a little higher and wider apart. She moaned as he drove his tongue inside her, fucking her with it as he fed. She arched her back, crying out. He had a thick tongue. It felt incredible.

He withdrew after a few minutes and zeroed back in on her clit. She felt oversensitive but he pinned her, not giving her a chance to wiggle away. Cathian had no mercy. He forced her to come again. Nara panted, trying to recover, but he fed off her, his tongue fucking her hard. Then again.

He was going to kill her by getting her off too many times in row! Though there were worse ways to go.

She smiled. It amazed her that the man gave her the best sex she'd ever had despite never actually putting his cock inside her. Even more amazing...the desire was there. Sometimes she wished he wouldn't use just his tongue to fuck her.

The human female cried out his name. Cathian eased his mouth off that little swollen bud that made her flood with the hormones he desperately needed. He lowered his mouth to her slit and pushed his tongue inside. She tasted sweet. His hunger began to abate, at least for now. He didn't want to stop though.

His dick ached, trapped between his belly and the bedding. But it wasn't time to purge. His balls felt heavy but he knew his seed wouldn't release yet. Going into heat had effectively stunned them into a state where sperm wouldn't leave until the hormone levels in his body reached peak breeding conditions. It didn't mean his dick didn't become painfully engorged.

The desire to fuck Nara was fierce, but he knew it would frustrate him and cause him more pain than pleasure. He'd never fed from someone from Earth, but if Nara was anything to judge by, humans were even more potent than Tryleskian women. The fact that he had the urge to drive his dick inside her even while starving for hormones was testament to that.

It also worried him.

What if he needed to purge his seed before the shuttle from his home world arrived? He knew the tight confines of Nara's pussy well, thanks to his tongue. His shaft was a lot thicker and would go far deeper inside her. He also had no idea how her body would react to his sperm when he released at the end of his heat cycle.

Tryleskian sperm during the heat could not only impregnate a female, but it also acted as a strong aphrodisiac. It sent females into instant heat, in order to withstand the hours it took to release all his stored seed into their bodies. He'd also become very aggressive. And she looked so frail to him.

He eased his tongue out and backed away from Nara. She seemed close to falling asleep. He'd exhausted her. Her chest rose and fell quickly, a fine sheen of sweat covering her pale skin. He gazed over her form. Her breasts looked delicate, and he knew they were soft globes. He'd explored them while feeding from her, enjoying the feel of them in his hands. She had very responsive nipples.

He turned away and walked to his desk, bringing up the computer screen from a hidden compartment. He listened to Nara's breathing slow, realizing when she fell asleep. He moved his fingers over the top of the desk once the keypad lit up. It didn't take long to log into the data they had on aliens, cross-referencing humans with Tryleskian.

There wasn't much to read.

Frustration had him biting back a snarl. According to the records, none of his kind had ever fed from or spent their heat with a woman from Earth. The lab reports stated they were compatible for feeding from, but it hadn't ever been tested on live subjects. He was the first to actually spend any part of his heat with a human.

A window popped up on his screen and he glanced at the message. Dovis wanted to speak to him. He agreed to meet his second-in-command outside his cabin in two minutes and shut off the monitor. It slid into the flat surface, the keypad fading from sight, and he quietly put on exercise pants. He didn't bother with a shirt or shoes.

Dovis paced in the corridor. His friend scowled. "I told Midgel and the Pods that the Earth woman wasn't good enough for you. I'm sorry they could only find you that one. I'll make this up to you somehow."

Cathian crossed his arms over his chest. "Make what up to me?"

"The woman isn't worthy of you. She's a criminal."

"I appreciate you looking out for me, but the auction house was the closest way to find a woman who couldn't refuse my need. Her crime was smuggling medical drugs. Not recreational ones that do harm. I believe her. Recreational sellers *use* their products. None are in her body, or I'd taste them."

"That still doesn't excuse Midgel and the Pods from buying you an unattractive alien. I don't know how you can stand to look at her."

He sighed. They had been friends for three years. He had grown to know everything about his second-in-command. Even his deepest secrets. "Stop. You only say that because of your people's history of hating those born in skin. Nara isn't unattractive. Don't project your issues on me—or her."

"That's not what I'm doing."

Cathian cocked his head, holding his gaze and refusing to blink.

Dovis looked away first. His shoulders drooped.

Cathian let it go. He'd made his point. "Anything to report? Any problems? Did anyone try to follow us when we left the auction? It's known for attracting all kinds, and some would love to attempt to steal this vessel."

Dovis held his gaze again. "It's all handled and running smoothly. The crew can survive without you while you suffer your heat. York has been very helpful and putting in extra shifts. Raff has as well. Your Pods are keeping to their cabin, occasionally monitoring your mental state. Marrow and Midgel are both fine. And Harver is keeping everything running. There's no need to worry. Just get through this ordeal."

"It's only a problem when I don't have a source to feed from." He smiled. "Now I do."

"We're right on schedule to meet up with the Tryleskian shuttle carrying the women from your planet."

"Good."

"Your father's assistant has assured me that he's bringing a prime selection for you to choose from. I'm sorry this happened. I should have paid more attention to your scent and noticed when it began to change."

"It's not your fault. Your job doesn't entail keeping track of my body."

"My sense of smell is keener."

"True, but I'm an adult. I know the signs. I ignored them when I stared to get irritable and distracted."

"This human is sufficient? You're getting what you need from her?"

"Yes. The crew did an excellent job of finding Nara. Please give them my thanks."

"Let's never do this again. Perhaps we should hire a Tryleskian woman to be on the crew full time."

"That will never happen. They don't leave the planet unless it's for short trips. Besides, I left my home world to *escape* all the women who tried to trap me into becoming their life-lock. A Tryleskian would see me as a prize to win."

"It wouldn't be a bad thing to have one, if you don't mind my saying so. She would have come in handy when you went into heat."

"A life-lock would mean having to return to live on my planet. I'm never going to end up like my father."

"Just because *he's* miserable doesn't mean you would be."

"I'm not willing to risk it. I want to find a woman who is drawn to *me*, instead of my family name and position. That's all Tryleskians care about. I could be ugly, maimed, and dishonorable, but they wouldn't care as long as they got to claim rights to me and our family fortune."

"I see."

"I need to sleep before the hunger returns and I lose my mind." He reached out, clasping Dovis on the arm. "Thank you. Give York my gratitude as well. Both of you are true friends."

"We've got everything handled. Just relax and get through your heat."

Cathian returned to his cabin, stripping off his pants. He crawled into bed, reaching for Nara. She murmured in her sleep but cuddled into his arms. He inhaled her scent, his hunger stirring. He ignored it as he tried to sleep. Heat was difficult on his mind and body, and he needed the rest.

Chapter Four

Nara panted, smiling. It was day two of being inside his cabin, and she'd already fed Cathian four times in a row that morning. Now he climbed up her body, pinning her under him.

He seemed to love to cuddle afterward, before he fell asleep. It had become a cycle with him. He fed a few times, until his hunger abated, then nap, waking when Dovis, the wolf-looking alien, brought them a tray of food. One time it had been a muscular blue alien man who she hadn't gotten a good look at. Cathian didn't allow them inside his cabin and always went to the door himself.

He surprised her when he leaned in close to her face, glancing at her lips. "I want to kiss you. May I?"

She didn't have to think about it. "Yes."

Cathian gently brushed his lips over hers, and she moaned softly. They were velvety soft but firm at the same time. His tongue met hers. She got a good hold on him, feeling the sharp tips of his fangs, but they didn't hurt. He tasted good, like the meal they'd recently shared. He growled, his chest rumbling against hers. He was a great kisser, passionate, and her body responded.

Eventually, he broke off the kiss. "What made you become a trader by career?"

His question surprised her, especially at that moment. She wanted to get back to kissing but he apparently wanted to talk. He usually slept after feeding, but his beautiful eyes weren't sleepy looking while she gazed into them.

"I wanted to leave Earth. There were a lot of painful memories."

"What kind?"

She debated on telling him or not and decided there was no harm. They were intimates, after all. "I was married, but it turned out that he wasn't the person I thought. It became ugly. He was a cheating, lying, thieving jerk."

His eyes widened.

"He slept with a couple of my friends behind my back. One of them got mad at him and told me. Everyone knew but me. I was an idiot who'd blindly trusted him."

"I read up on Earth. Married is a legal contract, correct? It's where both parties agree to terms."

"Yes."

"Was it a love match or business?"

"I thought he loved me but he didn't. Everything about him was a lie. He scammed me."

"Scam is to offer a high-quality product, but instead give an inferior one that has little to no value?"

She nodded. "That sums up my ex perfectly. I came with a lot of family money, and it turned out he just wanted *that* instead of me. He stole most of it, but I had some accounts hidden away. I divorced him and bought my shuttle. It's not much, a Dorkin Three model, but it got me off Earth and far from him. I didn't want to go to prison for murder."

He scowled. "You killed him?"

"No, but I wanted to. That was the problem. I would have if I'd stayed, and then would have been locked up for twenty years. He was mad when he found out I had secret accounts, and he couldn't touch them in the divorce. His way of retaliating was to harass and threaten me. It was best if I just disappeared where he wouldn't follow me. He'd never venture into space. It's too dangerous."

"You wanted a fresh start. I understand this."

"Is that why you're a captain? This seems like a big ship."

"It's a cruiser. I'm an ambassador for my planet. I mostly do trade negotiations and keep peaceful treaties active between my race and others. It got me off my planet."

"What's it like where you come from?" She felt very curious about him and his race.

"Beautiful but cold."

"Lots of snow?"

"No. Tryleskian is a warm planet all year round. Heavy in vegetation beyond our cities. The people are cold." He hesitated. "Most of our life-lock bonds are political in nature."

"You mean marriages?"

"Yes. I didn't wish to end up unhappy, the way my father and mother have. There is no love or even like between them. He chose her for her good looks and her family's history of being excellent breeders. She wanted his status and the perks that came with it. They are vicious and cruel to one another. Growing up with both together wasn't a happy childhood. I don't want my sons and daughters to be raised that way. Once I reached full maturity, it was my responsibility to breed the next generation or take this ambassador role."

"How long have you been doing it?"

"Three years."

"Do you like your job?"

"I do. Do you enjoy being a trader?"

She wanted to lie but decided not to. "Not really. It's scary most of the time. I lived in a human-only section of Earth. It wasn't by choice. It's just the way it is. Then I left, and suddenly I felt like I was lost out in space, you know? I hired two crew members. One is my navigator; she gets us where we need to go. She also speaks to all the aliens we sell to and deal with. She's half human and half Barcalon. They're good at learning languages. The other was the one who got us arrested, and he's fully human like me." She was still angry at him. "Derrick used the credits I gave him to buy hookers, instead of the part we needed for my shuttle. Our engine went down where we shouldn't have been after delivering medicine to a planet suffering Krout."

"The illness that turns bodies into vegetation?"

"Yes. They're a bunch of innocent colonists just trying to make a new life on a planet, but the space authorities want them gone. They shut down all travel there, including medical shipments that would cure them and save lives. I heard about it, and they were offering good money for anyone willing to risk getting past the blockades. So much for turning a profit and doing a good deed all at once. We got caught, and I picked being sold at the auction over going to Alto Prison."

"Good choice."

"That's what I was told by my crew. They said people are food there."

He lifted his chest off hers a little and glanced at her body, his scowl deepening. "You wouldn't have survived."

"Gee, thanks."

"I don't mean to offend you but your body is frail, Nara. You've seen other races. Yours isn't one with good defensive abilities in hand-to-hand combat."

She'd give him that. "True."

"You did a great service to me. A Tryleskian weakens from starvation during heat. It can take weeks to months to recover, depending on how sick he gets. There's also a risk of death if I'd gone into shock and my heart stopped. Thank you."

"No need for that. I was desperate. It was either say yes to the mouse woman from your ship, or get bought by a really scary red-skinned, horned guy who wanted to know if my blood was red." She shuddered. "I'm pretty sure you saved *my* life. I doubt I would have survived whatever he planned to do to me."

He nodded. "Never compare Midgel to a rodent within her hearing. She's sensitive about being teased. She's a sweet woman who prepares food for the crew. It was brave of her to go to the auction with a list of races compatible with mine. It went against her nature. She's timid, and doesn't leave her part of the ship. It was done out of pure loyalty to me."

"Sorry. I didn't mean to insult her."

"I know. You just need to be careful of what you say. I'm an ambassador. It's my duty to learn about other cultures. I've been reading up on Earth anytime I wake before you do."

"What have you learned?"

"Your people as a whole aren't liked by most."

"Fair enough." She had met a lot of people from her planet in space. "Most of the ones I've come across since leaving Earth aren't our best representatives. There are a lot of human slavers I've seen on various stations, selling other aliens. That's a death offense on my planet. It makes me sick."

"Because you are kind. You were arrested for trying to save lives."

"And make a profit."

He frowned. "Was it a rich colony planet?"

"No."

"Your profit margin would have been low, correct?"

She sighed. "I could make ten times more transporting slaves, but I flat-out refuse. I'd have probably set them free and earned a bounty on my head from their sellers or the buyers. My crew isn't happy about my ethics but it's my ship, my rules."

He lowered his chest against hers and slid his hand into her hair, stroking her scalp. She liked it when he did that. "You're a good human, Nara."

"You're a great Tryleskian, Cathian."

He chuckled.

* * * * *

Cathian had finished feeding from Nara and watched her fall asleep. He carefully extracted himself from bed and took a quick shower. He felt healthy and horny. His shaft remained hard and his nuts were uncomfortably swollen. His seed was still trapped in their sacks. It was a good thing. The idea of needing Nara for release frightened him.

He came out and went to his desk, contacting one of the scientists on Tryleskian. It took just minutes to get the expert he needed. Being a Vellar had its privileges. His family was one of the richest and most powerful on the planet.

The scientist stared at him from the screen. "Ambassador Vellar. It is an honor. What may I assist you with?"

"I've been accessing the database about our kind and humans."

The scientist frowned, looking puzzled.

"Earth," he added.

"Ah. Yes. I know of the planet and its inhabitants. We have done research on some who were arrested in our quadrant for trespassing without permission."

"Have any of our males been with one during our heat?"

"No. We only had access to their males and one female. She was life-locked to one of the males already. We took blood, fluid, and other samples before they were released. It's possible they are compatible but it hasn't been tested."

There went Cathian's hope that the database might be outdated.

"What is your interest, Ambassador Vellar? If you don't mind me being so bold as to ask."

"I went into heat earlier than planned and am currently sharing my heat with a human. She has strong hormone levels to feed me with."

Interest flared in the scientist's eyes. "That is fantastic news! Please have the onboard medic android take samples from her while she's aroused and freeze them for us. This is exciting."

The request frustrated Cathian. He didn't want to bring in the android to take samples from Nara. "In theory, would I harm her if I kept her until I released my seed?"

The scientist turned away, accessing something to the side. A good minute ticked away before he turned back. "In theory, perhaps. Their bodies are not as sturdy as those of our women. I've just looked at the imaging we took of the female we had in custody. I'm not certain a Tryleskian shaft would fit inside one, or if it would cause them damage. The female was life-locked to another human, as I stated, but the couple refused any sexual testing. Their males have smaller shafts than we do."

He ground his teeth together and bit back a snarl. "What about the chemicals we create when we release our seed? Would it act as an aphrodisiac for a human?"

"I'm not certain, Ambassador Vellar. Have the medic android save samples from you as well, when the time comes, and I'll personally run the tests myself when they are sent to me."

That wasn't going to help him. He'd only be able to get samples while releasing his seed. It would be too late by then to know what it would do to Nara if she were still with him.

"I am very enthusiastic about this opportunity. You're doing a brilliant job as ambassador for our planet." The scientist smiled wide. "You should take samples from all female races you come into sexual contact with. We will be able to exponentially increase our database."

"I won't have sex with different aliens for your research."

"That is a shame." He appeared disappointed.

Cathian fisted his hands. "Could I kill the human if I stayed with her through my heat? That's what I really need to know. You're the expert on this subject."

The scientist turned again to the other screen, taking longer that time to study the information he had on humans. He faced Cathian. "It's possible she may not survive. Her bone structure would be more delicate than that of our females. A Tryleskian shaft could cause internal damage, especially if maximum care wasn't taken. I'd say out of heat, it would safe. You could stop if you were harming her."

During his heat, he wouldn't be in control of his body when the time came to release his seed. That was the problem. He felt sick thinking about how badly he could possibly hurt her.

"I wouldn't suggest doing more than feeding from her if you care about this female, Ambassador Vellar. Take samples from her and send them to me immediately after your heat. I'll make it a priority. That way, you'll know if you can spend your next cycle with her."

"Thank you."

"Is there anything else you need, Ambassador?"

"No. That's it. Thank you for your time and immediate attention."

"Of course."

Cathian ended the transmission and walked over to the bed, staring down at Nara.

Her scent called to him. She was all he wanted. Not some other female. But he wouldn't risk her life.

Chapter Five

Nara climbed out of the tub and glanced at the closed bedroom door. The past five days had been a blur of oral sex, sleep, baths, and four regular meals brought to them by others.

It worried her to realize how eager she was to leave the bathroom and climb into Cathian's big bed.

She wanted him to touch her, certain she had become addicted to the big male...was maybe even falling in love with him. The drugs had long since faded from her system, no longer to blame for the way her nipples tightened just thinking about the Tryleskian male. He spoke to her between bouts of sleeping and licking her nearly to death. He was funny, intelligent, and incredibly sexy.

"Nara?" His gruff voice called out. "I'm hungry."

Her heart raced with excitement as she quickly dried off. "I'm coming."

He chuckled. "You will be. I need you."

She opened the door wearing a towel wrapped around her body and walked into the dim bedroom. He seemed to hate bright lights. The sight of a naked, aroused Cathian sprawled on his bed froze her breath inside her lungs. He had to be the sexiest, most beautiful man she'd ever seen. He'd showered before her bath and his hair had dried into a golden mane with red highlights, falling to just below his shoulders.

He patted his big mattress with a hand, his tongue wetting his lips. Heat radiated from between her thighs and she grew aroused with just that motion of his mouth. Her body's reaction confirmed that he affected her in ways no man ever had.

"You are sexy after bathing."

She doubted it. Her blonde locks were a mess of tangled wet hair. But she smiled. "Thanks."

His gaze narrowed. "Stretch out on your back and spread open for me." He swiped his tongue over his lower lip. "Feed me."

Two words had never turned a woman on more. She inched closer and then paused. "You said you were going to talk to Dovis when I took my bath. Did you?"

"Yes."

She stopped at the end of the bed. "What did he say?"

"The Tryleskian shuttle is within range. We'll dock with them in approximately ten hours."

And there will be women to take over his needs, she thought grimly. "What about me?"

An unknown emotion flashed across his features, tightening them before he relaxed. "You will be freed, money given to you, and then taken to the nearest space port. The bargain my crew made will be honored."

Something inside her chest broke…perhaps her heart.

Nara jerked her gaze from his, not wanting him to see how that information affected her. She wasn't ready to leave. She sure didn't want another woman in his bed, being touched the way he touched her, taking her place.

"Nara?" His voice softened. "Are you all right? I don't mind suffering hunger pains for a little while if you need to rest. I know you're not used to what I need from you."

It touched her that he'd care, proof of what a great guy he was, and she forced her gaze to his, seeing concern there. "I'm fine."

"Are you sure?" He sat up. "I've tried to restrain myself from taking too much from you."

She lowered her attention to his lap. His cock pretty much remained hard unless he slept, and often even then. His balls were red and swollen. It looked painful. "Does it hurt?"

He hesitated. "It's an ache that never stops."

She returned her focus back to his face. "You've never asked to enter me after that first day."

"There is no release for me yet, but soon it will be possible. I'm almost ready. I'm grateful the ship will dock with us soon. I've been afraid since last night that I'd hit the last cycle of my heat before they arrived."

"What happens when those women from your planet get here?"

"I will sniff them, decide by instinct which one will do, and then she will be restrained in here." A frown marred his lips. "Don't worry. You'll be put on a shuttle to be flown to a space port immediately after they arrive. You will be safe from me."

"Safe?"

He dropped his gaze to the bedspread. "Yes."

"Cathian? Please look at me."

He had a grim expression when he stared at her. "I'm going to want *you*. You're inside my blood, Nara. When the urge to release comes, it's *your* body I'm going to want under me."

His answer stunned her, but then she warmed inside at the omission. "I could—"

"No," he cut her off. "You can't."

"You don't know what I was about to say."

"Were you going to offer to stay here with me to complete the cycle?"

"Yes."

He moved on the bed, scooted off the end, and stood to his full height of six-foot-four. His muscles tensed as he faced her, the lines of them down his stomach rolling as he breathed. He took steps to close the distance between them. Nara tilted her chin up to keep their gazes connected.

"Do you see how much bigger I am than you?"

He was two of her, at least in body mass. "Yes."

"I will lose all control once I'm inside a female body, when I'm ready to release my seed. It's the heat. I'll…" He cleared his throat. "Do you know why they restrain the women? It must be that way for her safety. Males become aggressive if the females attempt to escape from them. Some have died by accident at the hands of a male if she tried to get away. I'll fuck until my knees collapse and every drop of the seed my body has stored has been released inside a female."

Nara had no words. It sounded as barbaric as he'd once mentioned.

His hand slowly reached up and cupped her cheek gently. "I'm afraid I'll hurt you. Tryleskian females enjoy the rough sex, and there is a chemical inside male sperm that creates an aphrodisiac, one that makes the shot my crew gave you feel tame in comparison. That's assuming your body reacts in the right way. It's never been tested with humans. I checked."

She let that sink in. "You did? Why?"

He glanced away before peering deeply into her eyes. "I wanted to know if it would be safe."

"You thought about asking me to finish your heat, didn't you?"

"Yes. I had hoped to discover success stories. That's not what I found. It's too dangerous, Nara. I won't risk your life. Males never remember the height of their heat or what they do. The pain is too intense and the instincts too great. You'll be dealing with…" Ae swallowed. "An out-of-control male bent on taking a woman until he collapses. It would be fucking, Nara. Not making love."

Just hearing Cathian saying that graphic word gave her a mental image of him entering her from behind, Nara tied down, and her body responded to that erotic image.

She saw his nostrils flare and he softly purred.

"You're starting to torture me, Nara. I smell you—and I want." He licked his lips. "Climb on the bed now."

Nara took off the towel and inched around the sexy male. She turned and sat on the edge of the mattress, spreading her thighs. Five days before, she'd have never done something so wantonly, but now she eagerly exposed her pussy to his view.

Cathian dropped to his knees and reached for her thighs. She loved when he purred, the way he did as he lowered his face to inhale her turned-on scent.

"Cathian?"

He glanced up. "What, Nara?"

"Can you enter me? I mean, just once? I want to feel you inside me."

He gaped at her. She could clearly identify his shock at her request.

"I know you can't come yet; I just want to know how it would feel."

He shook his head and straightened, staring into her eyes. "No. It will bring on the last cycle faster. I'm too close. The urge to be inside you grows stronger every day, and I wouldn't trust myself this close to the end of my heat."

It hurt that he denied her. Instead, some faceless woman would know the sensation of Cathian fully taking her body.

She lowered her chin, breaking eye contact, and lay back. She turned her head away to stare at the wall across the room, to make it impossible for her to see him.

"I understand," she whispered.

He didn't touch her. Seconds ticked by, the room unusually quiet.

"Nara?"

"What?"

"I want to. If you knew how strong the urge is to bury my shaft deep inside you, you wouldn't be disappointed."

It wasn't sexual disappointment she felt. It was the pain of rejection. But she'd never admit that to him. "It's okay."

Time passed and still she waited, but he didn't touch her. Curiosity finally forced her to look at him.

Cathian remained on his knees, watching her with an intense stare. He gripped her thighs, spread them wider—and then, to her surprise, moved his hips between her parted knees.

His cock brushed her pussy and his hands curled around the backs of her thighs, lifting them up his body to his ribs. He tugged until her ass hung off the edge of the bed.

"Just once, briefly," he rasped. "For us both. I long to feel you with more than my tongue and fingers."

He shifted his hips into position and the blunt tip of his thick cock bumped against the slick entrance of her pussy. He pressed against her more, slowly stretching her vaginal walls as he entered. Nara gripped his wrists just for something to cling to as he slid into her deeper. Pleasure at feeling his cock rubbing sensitive nerves had her biting her lip hard to keep her from asking for more.

Cathian's beautiful eyes closed and his head tipped back as he fully seated himself inside her welcoming body. It was a very snug fit. Nara couldn't look away from the pained expression that twisted his handsome features. Her hold on him tightened.

"Are you all right?"

"You're very tight, so hot and wet," he groaned. "I need to get out of you before I lose control."

She wiggled her ass, moving him inside her, and both of them moaned. His entire body tensed, his hold on her thighs tightened to near bruising, and then Nara did it again. She rolled her hips, loving the full, sensual feel of having his cock buried deep inside her pussy. She continued to move, fucking him slowly with the few inches his hold gave her to move against his strong body.

Sweat beaded his brow and his eyes squeezed shut as he started to growl and pant. Nara bucked on his cock, moaning at the ecstasy even the limited motion gave her.

"Nara, stop," he rasped.

"Please," she whispered. "Just fuck me a little. Move."

He lowered his head and his exotic golden eyes opened. "You want to know what it would really be like? I could lose control—it could bring on the end of my heat."

"Please? I'm willing to risk it, Cathian."

"You don't understand how rough I'll get. I'm being extremely gentle with you right now…"

"Please!" She held his stare, not looking away.

He snarled and yanked his hips back, withdrawing from her body abruptly.

Nara cried out in protest, ready to orgasm at that point. She didn't have time to voice her feelings because his hands slid to her hips. Nara gasped as the strong male flipped her onto her stomach and pushed her forward against the edge of the bed, bending her over it.

"You want me?"

She turned her head to stare at Cathian. Inches separated their bodies where he knelt behind her. "Yes."

"I'm sorry if this goes wrong."

"I'm sure it will be fi—"

Cathian entered her from behind, his cock driving into her pussy with one powerful thrust of his hips that pressed tight to her ass and pinned her firmly against the edge of the mattress. His hands left her body to grip her wrists, jerking them over her head and shoving them together. He adjusted his hold until his fingers shackled both wrists together, and then his free hand gripped her hip.

"I will try to remain in control."

She opened her mouth to tell him she believed he wouldn't hurt her, but then he started to fuck her, fast and deep.

Nara cried out in rapture as his thick, hard cock hammered her. Pleasure turned into pure bliss as she climaxed.

Cathian panted and stilled as her vaginal muscles clamped around his cock and she convulsed around him. He slowly withdrew from her pussy, and then collapsed over her. His hold on her wrist eased but he didn't let her go. Nara lay there trying to catch her breath, enjoying the feel of him pinning her down.

"Imagine hours of that," he rasped.

"I could take it."

He growled then released her as he straightened, backing away. "That was me being gentle. Roll over now and spread open for me. I need to feed."

She had to force her relaxed, limp body to move. It took a lot of effort, but she eventually ended up on her back. His strong hands lifted her legs and he hooked them over his shoulders before his face lowered. Nara smiled when he licked her, avoiding her clit.

He finally homed in on her clit, teasing her with his tongue to turn her on until she wanted to beg him to fuck her again. Instead, his lips sealed over the bundle of nerves and he sucked until an orgasm gripped her.

He released her with his mouth as he lapped up her release.

Time blurred as he fed from her, giving her ecstasy until he'd finally had enough. He shifted her legs, bent them up to her chest, and then collapsed on the bed next to her, rolling her onto her side. His muscular body curled around her. She loved it when he spooned her inside his tight embrace.

"The Tryleskian transport shuttle will arrive at the end of the sleep rotation. It will be goodbye." His arms tightened. "I will miss you very much."

Pain started in her chest and radiated outward. She clung to him. "It doesn't have to be that way."

"It does. You have told me about your shuttle on Frodder Planet, and you need to retrieve it before it's sold. Your crew members will meet you there if they were able to escape, and you will once again be free to be a trader."

Reality could be a horrible thing, but Nara knew he was right. She had a life she needed to get back to. She'd worked hard for a year and a half to make a career that earned her a decent living. It could be dangerous though, too, and she had already been arrested once. Of course, she'd learned to double-check to make sure her mechanic did as told, to prevent that from happening again in the future.

"Perhaps we'll meet again."

She doubted it. Cathian traveled great distances at times. She couldn't exactly chase after him in her smaller shuttle and find jobs at the same time to pay her crew.

"I hope so." She fought tears, not sure how someone could mean so much to her in five short days. But it happened. She lived and breathed the man behind her. He'd become everything to her. "I want to see you again."

"It was a bad time to go into heat, but I'm glad it happened. I never would have met you otherwise."

"I could stay until you're out of heat." She turned her head to peer into his exotic eyes. She could stare into them all day. "You're not going to hurt me."

"I won't risk it, Nara."

"It's my body, and I'm the one offering to be tied down." She smiled to soften her words. "That was pretty amazing while you were inside me. The idea of you doing that to me for hours doesn't sound bad."

"I would never forgive myself if I hurt you. I won't be in control. I know you don't understand, since humans are always in command of their bodies, but I'm not of your race. The urge overcomes everything when it begins. I'm an adult male, and I've survived many heat cycles. I remember being led to a female and the next thing I knew, I wake a day later in bed."

"Really?" She couldn't imagine.

He nodded. "Exhaustion afterward can last for up to twenty-four hours. I hear it is worse for the females. I'm not life-locked with one, obviously. I don't see the females afterward, since we're only together for the heat. If it could wipe me out, it must be extreme for them."

"Tell me more about being life-locked."

He frowned.

"Please?"

"It is a lifelong binding, when a couple joins together. Some alien races call it mating. They are inseparable until one dies, and usually the other follows closely behind. It is rare for a long-term couple to part and survive. I told you my parents are miserable. They can't get away from each other or they risk death."

"That could really kill them?"

He nodded. "It would be as though half your soul has left you, half your body ground to a halt. They lose their appetite, the ability to feel pleasure, since the only one they can get aroused for is no longer there, and there is no reason to live any longer."

"That sounds beautiful."

He snorted, shook his head, but then grinned. "Humans are strange."

"I mean the bond in general. Being the other half of someone's soul and being that dependent on each other."

"Are you forgetting what I've said about my parents? They aren't happy. They exist in two healthy bodies. They live to make each other miserable unless they are in bed. That's the only time they get alone. During sex."

"They don't love each other though. You said it was a political thing, right?"

"Yes. They are very different and share no common interests beyond my father wanting her to be the mother of his children, and her enjoying the status."

"What about love matches? I bet those relationships are spectacular when they life-lock."

"I've never met a Tryleskian pair that life-locked for love."

"Never?" That surprised her.

He shook his head. "I told you what my planet is like. The males deem beauty and the ability to bear children as top priorities. The females are looking for comfortable, pampered lives where others envy their statuses."

"You're telling me no men and women meet and fall in love? That's hard to believe."

He hesitated. "Our women don't work. They are pampered in homes with the children. Their lives revolve around shopping, buying comfort items they enjoy, and raising children. Once the female children reach adulthood, it's about finding a male with whom to life-lock. They are kept away from all males otherwise. A female who has sex outside of a life-lock would be less appealing to potential males of high status. There's no opportunity for the couples to meet until life-lock arrangements have been made."

"Wow."

It was the best thing she could think to say. Did Tryleskians not *allow* women to work? It sounded like a very male-dominated planet. The fact that women remained virgins while the men probably didn't offended her a little. Then again, maybe they were virgins too, since women weren't allowed to have sex until they life-locked.

"Imagine if your parents had liked each other though and got along."

He seemed to think about it. "My childhood would have been much happier. Speaking about childhoods, you don't talk of yours. What are your parents like?"

"They were happy together but they passed away."

"I'm sorry. Were you a child or an adult?"

"I lost them when I was eighteen. I'd moved out to live on my own and they began traveling. They wanted to see more of the planet. There was a train accident. Dad died instantly but mom lasted two days in the hospital before she succumbed to her injuries."

"That must have been difficult, but at least you weren't alone. I can't imagine the grief you must have felt."

"I *was* alone. And it was very difficult."

"Where are your littermates?"

"My what?"

He cleared his throat. "Siblings. I apologize. I read that humans don't give birth to litters. Just single births. You must have many."

"No. It's just me."

"That's impossible!"

"Earth is overpopulated, and you need permission to have a child. They usually only allow one per couple."

"On Tryleskian, I have many littermates."

"How many babies are born at once from a woman?"

"Two to five," he stated matter-of-factly. "Every three years, more of us were born, until my mother reached the age she could no longer conceive and my father's heat faded."

"Every three years…as in when your father went into heat?"

He chuckled. "Yes. Our planet thrives on life. It is the only time the male sperm is able to bring forth life inside a female."

"How many were born with you?"

"We were large male infants, so only three."

"Do they resemble you?"

He nodded. "We all look very similar."

"Right." She grew silent, thinking about how big his family must be.

"But you're alone." He gave her a sad look.

"I have my crewmates."

"One of whom lied to you by not fixing a broken part, and it resulted in your arrest." He nuzzled her head with his cheek. "I'll be in the Votor section in four months. That's close to Earth. I'd like to meet you there, Nara. I don't want our parting to be the end."

She grinned. He wanted to see her again. That meant goodbye wouldn't be forever. It made her feel a lot better; she felt heartsick about having to leave him. "I'd love that."

"Good. I have thought a lot about it," he softly admitted. "I just didn't feel right asking you because we'd have no future if you had to return to your family on Earth at some point. None of my travels take me there."

She reached up and rubbed his arm. It still bothered her that he refused to allow her to finish his heat cycle. The idea of him fucking another woman had jealousy burning through her gut.

Another thought struck, and she stilled her exploring of his skin.

"You can only get a woman pregnant while you're in heat?"

"Yes."

"Could you get the woman who will take my place pregnant?"

"I requested older females who are no longer able to conceive. If I were to impregnate one, I'd have to life-lock with her to ensure the future of our children. It's our law."

Nara gaped at him.

He nodded grimly. "I am hoping they managed to find females past breeding age."

Chapter Six

A bell stirred Nara from a deep sleep. The mattress moved as Cathian rolled away from her. Cool air hit her warmed skin where he'd been, and she shivered, burrowing into a ball. She heard his clothes rustle, and then the door opened. Her head jerked up as she came fully awake.

"They're about to dock," an unfamiliar female announced from the hallway. "I tried to contact you, but you didn't pick up, Captain Vellar."

"I was sleeping." He yawned, as if to prove his point. "I'll shower and then welcome the arriving party."

"I'm ready to take away the sex worker."

Cathian's entire body stilled and he snarled. "Don't call Nara that. She's much more."

Nara loved Cathian a little more for coming to her defense.

"Chill out. You are very grumpy when you're in heat. Your people brought five women with them, and they are eager for you to choose one. I'm not an expert on your heat, but I read up on it. You're only supposed to be with one woman. Are you going to try two this time?"

"Shut up, Marrow. You know my culture forbids that. It's offensive."

"Then get her out of your bed and cabin. I'm ready to take her away. I'll send in someone to change the bedding. Nothing pisses off women more than smelling the scent of another. I know you have a hyper-acute sense of smell, and so do your women."

Nara met Cathian's glance when he turned his head. Regret and dread filled her. She wondered what his thoughts and feelings were, unable to tell since he masked his features.

He addressed Marrow. "I'll meet them in the cargo bay when they land. Don't allow them onboard. Keep them contained there."

"Yes, Captain. What about the woman in your bed?"

"We'll shower, and she'll be ready to go when I leave my cabin."

"I'll just stand out here and wait then." Marrow snorted. "I'll hold up the wall."

"You do that."

The doors slid shut and he turned to face Nara. "It's time."

Tears burned behind her eyes. She hesitated and then pushed the covers off, rising naked from his big bed. She wanted to offer to stay again, but the night before he'd been clear that he wouldn't allow her to risk her life.

"You'll be safe with my crew, and they will take you to the nearest space port to find passage to retrieve your shuttle. I had Dovis issue you a card with many credits to make certain you have the ability to pay."

The sweet gesture made her love him even more. *Be brave*, she mentally ordered. Inside, she died a little, knowing that not only would she be leaving, but he'd completely forget her while he fucked some alien bitch, out of his mind from the heat.

"Let's shower."

She followed him quietly into the bathroom and they stepped into the large stall together. He waved on the water, which poured down to soak them. Hot tears spilled out and Nara turned her back to prevent him from seeing them.

His hand startled her when he gripped her hip. She turned in his direction.

Their gazes met, and then Cathian snarled, yanking her against his body.

She clung to him, crying while he hugged her. She didn't want to go. She really didn't want someone else touching him. What if he got the woman pregnant? If that happened, in four months she'd be waiting to meet up with him, and he'd never show. Or worse, he'd introduce her to his life-lock.

"Please let me stay," she whispered.

"Don't ask that of me again," he ordered softly.

"I can't help it!"

He rubbed her back, keeping her tight against his chest. Water poured down their bodies. "Four months will pass quickly."

"What if you get her pregnant?"

His entire body tensed. "Then I must do my duty to her and our children. I'd have no choice."

"You could let me—"

"No. I could never live with myself if I hurt or killed you."

Anger rose, and she pushed away, glaring up at him. "It's my life, *my* choice, and I'm willing to risk it!"

"I'm not."

"How would you feel if you knew I was about to fuck some other guy?"

He snarled, rage taking him over in a heartbeat. He fisted one of his hands and swung, punching the shower wall. The sudden show of violence startled her enough to jump and stare at his back, since he now faced away from her.

"I'd kill him."

She was stunned at the amount of jealousy his snarled tone implied. "Wow. I didn't expect such a strong reaction."

He spun to scowl at her and turned off the water. "I'm very possessive."

"So am I. Please don't make me leave! It is *killing* me knowing you're going to be with someone else."

"Damn it, Nara. We've been over this. You're the one I want, but it's too dangerous. *No.*"

They stared at each other. Tears filled her eyes and she opened her mouth to argue with him again. He cut her off before she got a word out.

"It's too great a danger. I won't remember what I do to you, will lose the ability to think at all while gripped by the end of my heat. I'm barely able to stay in control now."

"I get that. You just punched a wall. I'm grateful it wasn't me."

"I would never hurt you. That's why you must leave."

"You said you black out. I assume your body would just take over. I'm still willing to risk it."

He closed his beautiful eyes briefly, then opened them. "I go feral. I'm dangerous when it begins. I could accidentally kill you, Nara. I'm afraid it would hurt you enough that you'd put up a fight. I warned you that women have died that way. I *will not* risk your life, Nara. We'll leave it to fate and hopefully, in four months, we'll meet again."

"Damn it, Cathian! Say we do it your way? What if we meet up in four months and we don't want to be apart again? You'll go into heat in three years. Do you expect me to just step aside and let you fuck one of your women then too?"

He stared into her eyes and a look of misery etched his handsome face. "I'm hoping there's more available data by then. Maybe one of our males will spend his heat with a human and document it. We could also visit my planet to have them run tests on us. I refuse to allow you to be the first…like some test subject."

"I have feelings for you. Do you understand that?"

"I won't risk your life."

"But—"

"I have feelings for you too, damn it!" He snarled, looking enraged. "But you are *not* staying. I won't take the chance I might kill you. It's time for you to leave."

She knew the subject had ended for him as he pulled away and stepped from the shower. Depression hit her hard as she turned off the water and dressed in clothing provided for her by the crew. Cathian had made up his mind and nothing would change it.

She kept her dignity in place when he opened the door and allowed a crew member inside his cabin to strip his sheets and remove all traces of her. Marrow waited at the door to lead her away. She was a type of alien Nara couldn't identify, but she looked buff for a woman. Her skin was a light brown and a soft layer of tiny hair, like fuzz, covered every revealed inch of her body, including her face.

"About time," the woman muttered. "Let's go to the shuttle."

Nara met Cathian's intense gaze, but then he looked away, turned his back, and stormed out of his cabin. She watched him go and pain stabbed at her chest. He didn't glance back once, disappearing around a curve and out of sight.

"Follow me," Marrow ordered gruffly. "You need to be long gone by the time he returns. He won't be alone."

Ouch. Rub it in, why don't you? Bitch. Nara glared at her.

"Yeah, yeah," Marrow sighed. "Our captain is hot. I'm feeling zero pity for you. He won't touch any of the crew. I've tried more than once to get a ride on that fine piece of male specimen, and you got to spend almost a week getting licked by him. It's time for you to get off our vessel. Move or I'll drag you."

Nara fought tears. She didn't want to leave. Marrow began walking in the opposite direction Cathian had gone. It was tempting to run after him and beg him to change his mind. He wouldn't though. And it hurt. She forced her legs to move and followed the alien woman.

"I'm going to pilot you to the Tabus station. Ever been there before?"

"Yes."

"Great. Then I don't have to talk you through the best places to stay and how to get a shuttle to wherever it is you want to go next. York told me to do that."

"Who's York?"

"The only Parri on this vessel."

"I don't know my alien races."

"He's huge and blue."

"I glimpsed him once but that was it. He delivered food to the door."

"He's a pain in my ass today, but he's a great fuck. Now *he* doesn't turn down crew members."

Nara let that slide, grateful Cathian hadn't ever bedded the woman. She followed the taller female through the corridors until they came to a docking sleeve. The doors were open. The shuttle waiting for them was tiny, with just two seats. They weren't even side by side, but one in front of the other. Marrow pointed to the one in the back.

"There's credits and a change of clothing inside the bag on the floor." She jerked her thumb. "Sit, and we'll be at the station within a few hours. I'm a great pilot. Don't look so frightened. You aren't going to puke, are you?" Marrow curled her lip. "Please don't. I'll be annoyed. I'd have to clean it up."

"I'm not afraid."

"You're pale, and you look ill."

"It's stress," she admitted.

"These small transport shuttles are safe. I fly them all the time to pick up supplies with York." Marrow dropped into the front seat. "Strap in tight. The compartment might be cramped but we've got powerful engines and thrusters. I don't want you getting hurt by being stupid."

Nara put on the belts to secure her body to the seat and winced when they jettisoned from the larger ship. It wasn't the violent motion, but more from the turmoil she felt inside.

Right now, Cathian is meeting those women. Picking one. Damn. It made pain stab her chest and jealousy became a literal burning sensation inside. *I don't need him. I don't. My life was fine without him.*

She tried to remember that. First, she needed to get to her shuttle before it was sold, hope that Derrick had escaped, and that he showed up with the part. They'd be able to take off from Frodder Planet, and Belinda would hook them up with their next job. Derrick will have learned his lesson, and they'd never find themselves dead in space again to be arrested when they had a less-than-legal shipment. Nara rubbed her fingers on her pants and chewed on her bottom lip.

Yeah, always worrying about whether I'll be arrested or killed if a trade goes wrong. I could end up stranded in space again. On another auction block, or worse, that killer planet where the prisoners would eat me.

She pushed those thoughts back. She had a good life she'd worked hard for. She'd be fine.

Lonely, sleeping on a narrow bunk while dwelling on how much I miss Cathian. Remembering the time we spent together.

She closed her eyes and his image instantly surfaced. His laugh would haunt her, the memory of his warm body curled around hers, and that sexy, deep voice of his.

There was more she'd miss. He had a quick sense of humor but an intensity that was just as appealing. He was the kind of man a woman could happily spend her life with. He wouldn't cheat on her if they life-locked. She'd be the other part of his soul, his other half. She yearned for that. He'd make life interesting. Every three years, he'd go into heat and nearly lick her to death.

The memories she'd made with him flashed through her thoughts.

She tried to focus on the idea of being pregnant with three to five babies as a reason to be glad she was leaving him behind. But instead of feeling relieved, she reached down and touched her stomach.

Who was she kidding? She'd love to carry as many little Cathian babies as possible.

She loved him.

It hit her like a sledge hammer. She couldn't lose him, no matter what it took. He might knock up that woman sharing his heat.

It wasn't happening. If any woman was going to carry his litter, it would be her.

"Turn the shuttle around. We need to go back."

Marrow twisted her head to gawk at her over the pilot seat. "What?"

"Turn us around. I'm going back to Cathian."

Marrow shook her head and faced forward. "No, you're not. Captain doesn't want you. You're just a sex worker. The money is in the bag at your feet. Services paid. I'm taking you to the Tabus station; and that's the *only* place you're going."

Nara's eyebrows arched. "I can't talk you out of it?"

"No. The captain doesn't want you anymore."

Nara swiftly unbuckled her belt and stood, tightly wrapping her arm around the pilot's neck.

Marrow gasped, but with her belt on as she fought to pry Nara's arm loose, it kept her from doing little more than jerking in her seat until she lost consciousness from lack of air.

Marrow weighed a ton. Nara had to struggle to lift her out of the pilot's chair, and then just dumped her on the narrow strip of floor to the side of the seats. She grabbed the bag, removed the strap from it, and used it to firmly tie Marrow's hands behind her back.

She dropped into the pilot's seat and softly cursed. It wasn't a model she'd ever learned to fly. Her shuttle was much bigger. "How hard can it be?"

Minutes later, she'd turned the shuttle around and was flying back toward the blip on the scanner that acted as a homing device for the transport.

"I'm coming, Cathian."

* * * * *

Cathian didn't hide his frustration and anger from Rex. "I specifically requested older females who are past fertile age!"

"I apologize, Ambassador. Your father personally picked all five of these women." Rex smiled and leaned in, softening his voice. "He wants you to retire from this post. Your brother Dax has requested to take over your current work for our planet."

He gritted his teeth. His father had pressured him before to return to Tryleskian, mentioning he had one of his brothers in mind to fill his position. Cathian had adamantly refused. He loved being an ambassador and traveling. His crew had become a secondary family he enjoyed spending time with. Dovis and York, his best friends, would hate living on Tryleskian. They might even refuse to return with him.

His younger brother Dax could find something else to do if he wanted off their planet. He wasn't getting his job.

"Your father believes you are at an age where you should be life-locked and breeding. You can't blame him. I believe you are his favorite. Cavas has refused to leave his military service. Crath hasn't returned home from his cultural research or contacted your parents in months. It's understandable that one of you three should be responsible and do your duty. You are the firstborn in your litter, and the oldest of all the children. It's time for you to settle down and breed a new generation for your family."

"My father is punishing me for my littermates defying him? *No.* I refuse to allow it. You can inform my parents that Crath is fine. I spoke to him weeks ago. And I don't blame Cavas for sticking with his military service. He loves to fight."

Rex stepped next to him and motioned toward the women staring at them from across the cargo hold. "Inspect them. They are waiting."

Cathian grimaced as he looked toward the five young Tryleskians waiting for his attention. He knew the reason for their eager expressions wasn't due to being off the planet and on *The Vorge*. They were imagining landing his fortune and status if he got one of them pregnant.

It would be his parents all over again. He'd be miserable.

His father would only send women who were fertile, who had mothers and probably older sisters who'd conceived during the heat.

The urge to flee hit hard. As if his father's assistant could read his thoughts, Rex spoke.

"They were medically scanned before we left our planet, and they come from between the fourth and sixth litters of their parents. Notice the one on the far left has exceptionally wide hips? The women in her line are known to carry at least four to five infants at a time. And the one with the lightest hair, every woman for five generations has conceived during heat without fail. She is a guaranteed success."

Cathian closed his eyes, feeling sick to his stomach. A throbbing sensation inside his chest came next. Nara filled his thoughts as the memories they'd made together replayed in his mind. Her smile, her laugh, her gaze locked with his. The way her fingertips lightly stroked his body and how good she felt in his arms. The memories haunted him. The sound of her voice was something he already missed, despite sending her away little over an hour ago.

He'd gone to the bridge before venturing to the cargo hold to face Rex and the women, to speak with Dovis and track Nara's transport.

And to stall. He admitted being guilty of that. The thought of touching anyone but Nara didn't appeal to him. He'd hoped to waste time until the progression of his heat gave him no choice.

Only the thought of seeing Nara again in four months had given him the ability to walk away from her. He'd even had York pack her a detailed travel plan for *The Vorge*, to make it easier for her to find him in case they missed their meeting.

A meeting that wouldn't happen. His father had made certain of that by picking these women.

Pain burned hotter inside his chest. He'd never be able to see Nara again, forced to life-lock to whichever female he chose. She would get pregnant and birth his litter. He'd be stuck with one of these five for the rest of his life. It would be miserable, and he'd live with the knowledge that he had been happy once inside his cabin with a sexy, sweet human who had claimed his heart.

"Ambassador," Rex whispered. "They are waiting to be inspected. You don't look well. You're unusually pale, and you're trembling. There's no need for you to suffer any longer. It's time to complete your heat cycle."

He ignored him.

Rex touched his arm. "Cathian, I've known you since you were a boy. You've always been stubborn but it's time to return to our planet and start breeding the next Vellar generation."

Cathian jerked away and opened his eyes.

He wasn't going to allow this to happen. Perhaps if he'd never met Nara, spent so much time getting to know her, he'd have accepted his fate. But now...

"Take them all and return to my father. Tell him I refuse to allow him to manipulate me."

Rex's eyes widened, and he gasped.

"You heard me."

"You're irrational. It's the heat you're suffering. You know your body can't withstand not completing your cycle without grave or possible deadly consequences."

"I've been feed well. I'm strong. I won't die."

"Your body will go into shock and you'll get sick, if your heart can even withstand the agony. You'll go insane at the very least, and attack a female member of your crew."

"That's why I'm going to have Dovis and York chain me down in my cabin and drug me."

He spun away, moving toward the cargo doors. He'd rather risk his health and life than give up meeting Nara in four months. He also made a mental note to have the vessel's automated medical android take samples of his sperm to test on Nara. That way, he'd know during his next heat cycle if it would act as an aphrodisiac for her or not.

"Cathian!"

He ignored Rex's shout, and almost reached the doors when something painful pierced his shoulder blade.

He froze for a split second—and then twisted his head, reaching back. He yanked out the dart embedded into his skin, spun, and glared at his father's assistant. The male held a weapon he must have hidden in the back of his uniform waistband.

"What did you do?"

Rex looked nervous. "Your father knows you well. I'm sorry. He suspected you might become angry and defiant. We took precautions."

"I'm going to kill you!" He took a step toward Rex, but suddenly his knees gave out beneath him and slammed into the metal plating of the floor. Spots appeared before his eyes and he fought to draw air. His heart raced.

"I apologize, but this is for the best." Rex stayed back, not drawing within arm's reach. "It will knock you unconscious for a short period of time, and when you wake, you won't be rational. You'll only be able to listen to your body's needs. I'll chose the lightest-haired female for you. She'll provide you many beautiful sons and daughters."

A roar filled his throat but only a whimper escaped his parted lips as he pitched forward. He didn't even feel it when he crumped all the way onto the deck. He *did* hear Rex's voice though.

"Now to get him to his cabin. Vis, I pick you. Come with us."

Chapter Seven

It surprised Nara to realize how far the shuttle had traveled from Cathian's ship before she'd decided to do whatever it took to get back to him. He was definitely worth fighting for. She only hoped she'd reach him before he lost his mind and touched some female Tryleskian.

Worry ate at her that he'd be mad, would flat-out refuse again to take her instead of risking her life, but she just wouldn't take no for an answer. He'd have to physically pick her up and fly her to the station himself. Of course, him being in full heat would make him want to touch her. He couldn't fly and do that at the same time.

"You're mine," she swore aloud. "Not someone else's. I won't risk losing you...and I have a feeling you've got powerful sperm."

Besides dealing with Cathian's reaction when she confronted him, it might be tough to get past his crew. She remembered the way to his cabin from where they'd boarded the transport, but his crew might try to stop her. A check of the flight logs revealed the autopilot would dock them in the same location.

Marrow woke slowly. "What have you done? You're stealing from the captain? I knew you were a criminal!" The woman struggled on the floor.

"I'm not stealing. We're returning to *The Vorge*. "

"Why?" Marrow fought the strap binding her wrists behind her back and tried to get up from the floor. The space was too cramped, and she just ended up rolling from the door up against the bottom of the seats.

"Cathian was afraid to finish his heat with me. I'm not going to let some cat woman from his planet have him. Did you know he has to marry her if she gets pregnant?"

Marrow suddenly stopped struggling. "What?"

"He asked for older women who can't have babies, but I had a friend who was a late-in-life, whoops baby."

"I don't know what you mean."

"Her mother had hit menopause and didn't have a period for over a year. Then she found out she was pregnant. It's rare but it happens. What if the same thing happens to the woman he picks? It's like a law to his people that if you knock someone up, then you're stuck with them for life."

"Shit," Marrow said.

"I know. You already admitted you want him but…sorry, not happening. I'm too attached to him."

"It's not that. Mated males from their planet always return home to live there. Their females are highly spoiled and enjoy being close to family. That's why you won't see many females at stations or on planets unless they're on vacation. They don't enjoy leaving their home world, and most just stubbornly refuse.

"It means we'll lose our captain, and the Tryleskians will send someone to replace him. I've been arrested for fighting a few times. The captain was willing to overlook it after I explained. I doubt others would even bother to ask my reasons. Cathian is easygoing but most Tryleskians are known to be strict."

Nara saw an opportunity. "You could help me get to him once we dock. I've been worried about the crew trying to stop me. Will you help?"

"Never." Marrow glared at her. "It doesn't matter which woman he releases his seed into. *You* could get pregnant by him. He'd still give up his ambassador title and return to his planet. I'd have a new boss who would fire me and kick me off *The Vorge*."

"You're forgetting that I'm not a Tryleskian. I don't care *where* I live and I have no interest in moving to his planet. I just want to be with him."

Marrow frowned, studying her. "You'd allow him to remain captain?"

"Yes. I just want *him*. I bought a shuttle and left Earth to live in space. Your vessel is much larger than what I'm used to. I'd be perfectly happy on *The Vorge*."

Long seconds ticked by. "Release me. I'll help you get to the captain's cabin and prevent any of the crew from stopping you."

Nara hesitated. "How do I know I can trust you? That you won't just knock me out and I'll wake up on the station?"

"I need this job." Marrow held her gaze. "I'm a Sarrin. Women on my planet are required to be submissive to all males. We're treated like shit. I suffered countless beatings from my father for being too strong-willed before I ran away and escaped onto a transport leaving my world. I am *never* going back. I plan to stay on *The Vorge* until I find a suitable mate—when I'm *ready* to take one. Not because I'm forced to."

Nara still wasn't convinced.

"I'm happy here. This is the first vessel I've ever worked where I'm treated as an equal. I never fear being attacked by my own crew, either.

They give me respect. The captain sends York with me to pick up supplies to make sure no one messes with me. I'm protected. That's priceless. Out here alone, women are targets for slavers."

That struck a nerve with Nara. "I know. I understand. I left Earth alone, and I've seen some really bad things." She leaned over the seat and began to untie the belt holding Marrow's wrists together. "Just don't be a liar, Marrow. Cathian means everything to me."

The other woman rubbed her wrists when she was freed and stood. "We'll only have a problem if you get pregnant and demand the captain returns to his planet to live. Then I will beat you."

"No worries. His planet doesn't appeal to me."

"Now get out of my seat. I'm the pilot."

Nara moved out of the way to let the woman pilot the shuttle. Marrow didn't change course, and Nara relaxed. "Thank you."

"I have my own selfish reasons to return you to the captain."

"Will security show up at the sleeve when we dock, since you're not due back for a while?"

"I'll handle them. There are only nine crew members. They will stand down when I order them to. I'm trusted. And none of them want things to change."

"I just hope we get there in time."

"Hold on."

Nara was thrust back against her seat a split second later. She smiled. Of course the pilot would have the codes required to override the transport computer and fly faster than deemed safe.

"Thank you."

"Stop saying that. It's annoying. Don't expect me to be your friend if you stay either. I don't like girl discussions."

"Understood."

Time seemed to crawl but then Marrow slowed them and began docking procedures. The engines shut down, and Marrow unbuckled while Nara did the same. Their gazes met as they stood.

"I go first. You stay behind me. We haven't spoken about what to do with the Tryleskian female if she's already inside the captain's cabin. None of the crew would dare touch her. It's a violation of our work contract to attack one in any way. We represent their planet."

"I'll wing it."

"What does that mean?"

"It means I don't know what I'm going to do, but I'll figure it out once we know what the situation is. Just get me to his cabin."

Marrow opened the door and strode through the sleeve, Nara on her heels.

They didn't make it more than ten feet inside before Dovis confronted them. He held a weapon.

"What is going on?"

"Stand down," Marrow ordered him. "Trust me. She needs to get to the captain."

"No." He snarled and came closer, glaring at Nara.

Marrow grabbed his shirt and pressed against him. "We'll lose Captain Vellar if he gets one of his kind pregnant. Nara is human. She promised to let him stay onboard. Can you say with certainty that his replacement will keep you on? Do you have a desire to go live on his planet in order to stay with him? What would you do? Perhaps take a job as an infant sitter for his children?"

Dovis growled deeply, looking furious. "No to all."

"Then step aside and let us pass."

"She's weak. I doubt she could carry his offspring."

"Exactly." Marrow gave him a shove and snorted. "Even better. Can you say the same for a Tryleskian female?"

Dovis shook his head but he holstered his weapon. "Cathian could kill her. Then he'd blame *me*. He's *fond* of her."

Nara wanted to roll her eyes. "No need to sneer when you say that word. Geez. I don't know why you dislike me so much, but just tell him I forced you."

"Is that a joke, human?" Dovis flashed fangs at Nara. "That's an insult to me. You couldn't make me do anything."

She held out her hand to him. "Give me your weapon. I won't shoot you; I'll say I stole it. I'm so pathetic you didn't think I'd make a grab for it. Being shot would take you down, right?"

"I would never give you a stunner." He grabbed it and yanked it from the holster and, to her surprise, offered it to Marrow. "*You* shoot me."

Marrow hesitated.

"Someone needs to stun me. And I don't trust *her*." He tossed his head in Nara's direction. "Anything less than being knocked out would be unforgivable to Cathian."

Nara grabbed the weapon before he could react and shot him in the chest. "We don't have time for this."

He staggered back, his eyes wide, and then fell over backward. His body made a loud thump when it hit the deck.

She winced. That would leave some marks and bruises. He'd fallen like a brick.

"He's going to be very angry when he comes around," Marrow whispered. "You shouldn't have done that."

Nara kept the stunner. "I might need this. Let's go!"

"Shit. I'm going to get fired."

"No, you won't."

The quiet voice made both of them jump and turn.

The three Pods had crept up behind them. One of them smiled.

"The captain is inside his cabin. His mind is lost to need at the moment, but he's fighting it. The female chained to his bed doesn't smell right to him, but his pain is intense." He looked at Nara. "I'm glad you returned. We'll tell him we witnessed you stealing Dovis's stunner. You did, after all."

"She did," another one agreed. "Don't shoot us. Go. Hurry."

"We have the rest of the crew distracted. Your path is clear," the third one informed her.

Nara turned and bolted towards Cathian's cabin. She reached it, panting, and tried to get in. The door refused to open.

"Shit!"

"I've got this."

The deep voice startled her. She twisted, raising the weapon.

The huge alien behind her grinned, showing off two large fangs. He reminded her of a vampire on massive steroids that had been dipped in blue paint. His black hair was a stark contrast to the lightness of his body color.

"Don't shoot, little human. I have access to the door lock. I brought you food, remember? Do you want in?"

"Yes."

"I'm York. You're Nara. The Pods picked up your thoughts when you came into their weird head range they have. It was before you docked. They knew I'd help, since I like to break rules. Stand aside and let me get the door open. Those assholes from his planet drugged Cathian with something to escalate his heat, or some such shit. The Pods alerted us as it was happening, but we arrived too late to do anything about it. Captain was mindless, snarling, and he couldn't give us orders. That shaft-head Rex said he'd die if we didn't let him chain the woman inside and let the captain at her."

Nara kept the stunner trained on him but gave him room to reach the panel. "Please open it."

He gave a sharp nod but gave her a wide berth. "Once it's open, shoot me. Then I can say I was forced too." He chuckled. "And I could use a nap. But let me lie down first." He reached up and tapped a device on his ear. "Marrow says there's a huge lump forming on the back of Dovis's head. He really is going to be pissed at you when he wakes."

The door opened, and York backed away fast, dropped into a crouch, and then rolled onto his side on the floor. "Shoot!" He actually sounded excited.

She fired the stunner, nailing him in the hip. He jerked once but then slumped.

Nara rushed inside the cabin before the doors could auto seal. They did so immediately once she was clear of them. The interior was much dimmer than normal, and it took a few blinks of her eyes to adjust, enabling her to see.

The scene inside stunned her.

A big-boned, cat-looking female had been bound naked against the side of the bed, her arms outstretched toward two posts, her knees spread and secured to the bolted legs of the bed. She hissed at Nara from her position.

"Who are you?" The woman sounded and looked pissed.

A deep growl answered, making Nara jerk her head to the corner of the room at the other side of the bed.

An equally naked Cathian crouched there, his beautiful gaze fixed on Nara. He had a purely animalistic appearance—but the truly terrifying part was that she didn't see any recognition in his eyes as he glowered at her.

She hesitated a second before pointing the stunner at the woman, still hissing and snarling at her.

She fired, hitting her in the ass. The woman slumped against the bed.

"I hope that wasn't against the law. Ignorance is bliss, right?" Her gaze locked on Cathian. "Hi, sexy. I'm back. Did you miss me? I missed you."

His nostrils flared as he sniffed, and he growled low. It was a dangerous sound. His body tensed, and he suddenly dropped forward on his hands and knees.

She glanced at the weapon in her hand but then tossed it away, reaching for her clothes instead, wanting to get them off.

Cathian slowly crawled toward her on all fours. He looked more cat than man at that moment. It was still sexy as hell. She inched to the side, heading toward the bathroom. They needed privacy. She didn't want that cat woman waking up and yelling at her for shooting her in the ass, or worse, interrupting them.

"Easy, baby. Don't leap at me and take me down like a deer, okay? That's what cats do, right? Let's go somewhere we can lock in together in case your unwanted guest gets free."

Cathian sniffed at her again, and this time a loud purr came from him. She smiled as she threw off her shirt, the toed off her shoes as she kept moving. He followed her through the bathroom door, where she shoved down her pants and underwear. He growled.

"Close and lock the door."

He didn't move, watching her.

"Okay." She wasn't going to try to get past him to do it herself. His body looked tense and he was breathing hard. He really did look like he was about to lunge at her. He still didn't appear to really know who she was. He wasn't speaking, either. "The bed is taken. This will have to do."

She reached up and licked her finger, lowered her hand, and then began rubbing her clit.

He snarled and crawled closer.

Nara turned, saw her pale reflection in the mirror, and admitted she looked a bit afraid. She shoved that emotion back as she furiously rubbed her clit, needing to get turned on. Otherwise, she knew it would hurt when he took her. He'd told her enough times what was going to happen at the end of the heat. That moment had arrived.

She used her free hand to snatch the towels hanging on the hooks next to her and shoved them over the curved edge of the counter. It should cushion her a little at least. She kept her hand moving all the while, continued to manipulate her body. Her eyes closed as pleasure worked its way through her.

Cathian's strong hands suddenly grabbed her hips and shoved her roughly against the counter.

She gasped, opening her eyes.

He wasn't standing but instead was on his knees behind her. She couldn't see his face. Her body was in the way. He shoved her higher, and she threw out her arm to protect her face from slamming into the mirror as he bent her over the counter. Hot air fanned her pussy, and then his nose brushed against her sex. He sniffed and growled.

"It's me, sexy."

He licked her, and she struggled a little to free her other hand, finally pulling it up and bracing her arms against the counter and mirror to protect her body. Cathian licked at her clit, and she forced her body to relax. She loved that tongue. He usually teased her a bit with it, but not at that moment. Pleasure had her moaning and pressing her forehead against the arm resting on the cold glass in front of her. She came fast, crying out his name.

He snarled and released her hips. She lifted her head, saw him stand behind her, and met his gaze in the mirror. He looked away, staring down at her ass as he spread his legs a bit, moved closer to her, and grabbed her hips again.

"That's it, Cathian. Take me."

He didn't hesitate, and she cried out as he drove into her.

There was nothing gentle about the way his thick cock breached her, but she was soaking wet. It didn't hurt so much as stun her to have him buried deep inside so suddenly. He gripped her flesh in a bruising hold and she lowered her head, pressing it against her arm again. He almost completely withdrew from her before slamming back home.

She moaned and he snarled, getting a better grip on her hips. His cock felt incredibly hard.

Suddenly he froze—and then Cathian buried his face against her neck, his hips hammering, fucking her furiously. Pleasure built from the manic friction he created against sensitive nerve endings.

He snarled again, threw back his head and roared.

She could feel every hot jet of his semen as he filled her, sending her over the edge into climax, and she gasped when his big body shook from the force of his release. She panted with him, knew she'd have bruises, but she didn't care.

A cramp suddenly hit her belly, and a fire seemed to spread through her limbs. Her eyes widened as her nipples tightened painfully. A wave of passion gripped her until she wiggled frantically on the cock that still impaled her.

"Please," she begged. "More!"

Cathian began to fuck her again, hard, deep, and the pleasure grew until she was grateful he held her pinned over the counter. Her knees wouldn't hold her weight. Another climax hit Nara, and Cathian roared out again, his big body quaking as he came as well. More heat spread, the fire burning brighter, and she understood that his sperm affected her the way it must affect Tryleskian women. He'd been right when he said the chemical his body made worked better than the drug she'd been given by the crew. She urged him on again by rocking on his cock.

"More."

His head lifted from her neck and their eyes met in the mirror. The wild beauty of him nearly made her come. This time his golden eyes held hers while he slid an arm around her waist, anchored her tighter against his body, and continued to fuck her.

Time blurred, the pleasure grew ever more intense. There was nothing but Cathian, and the bliss as he made her orgasm over and over.

Chapter Eight

Nara became aware of a big hand rubbing her ass and a firm, warm body curled around her back. She opened her eyes to find she lay on Cathian's bed. She turned her head to peer at him.

He watched her with his hand propping his head up.

She tried to remember how they'd gotten back into the main part of the cabin but couldn't. They'd been in the bathroom, going at it against the counter numerous times, but at some point had ended up on the floor. Snatches of memory came of him on top, riding her over and over. Her entire body ached. She knew she'd have tons of bruises, and there was a definite throbbing between her legs. She was beyond tender.

She smiled.

He didn't smile back. His eyes were intense, beautiful, but his features didn't show his emotions. "How are you feeling?"

"Sore but happy. How did we get here from the bathroom?"

Instead of answering, he scowled. "You're black and blue on your ass, back, and the front of your hips." Regret filled his expression. "My handprints are bruised into your hips."

"Ah. It's fine." She gently eased away from him and rolled so they were facing each other.

He sat up and scooted until he rested his back against the headboard. His gaze locked with hers. "You got me through the end of my heat. How? I sent you away."

He didn't remember anything. "That's kind of a story. Probably not one to tell you right now."

"Nara." His voice deepened.

She sighed and sat up too. He glanced down her body, and flinched. She followed his gaze, inwardly wincing a little as she saw the black and blue marks. "I'm *fine*." She looked up at him. "More than fine. I survived. Oh, and your sperm totally works on me like it would one of your women."

He reached up and cupped her face. "Nara, I'm trying not to lose my fucking mind here. I woke up to find you battered to hell in my bed. You're supposed to be *safe*. Instead, I realize..." He pulled her closer and leaned forward until their faces were inches apart. "I could have killed you."

"You didn't."

He opened his mouth, closed it, and growled low.

"Here's the highlights. Ready?"

"Tell me."

"I choked Marrow until she blacked out in the shuttle, tied her up, and returned to your ship. I know how to fly a shuttle; I'm a pilot too. Then I shot both Dovis and a big blue guy. Oh, and that woman chained to your bed."

His eyes widened, and he paled.

"They're alive. It was just a stunner. I stripped off my clothes and lured you into the bathroom." She smiled then. "I wasn't going to risk losing you forever."

"Nara, what were you thinking? I could have killed you!"

"I'm alive. And I was thinking I refused to lose you to some other woman. It's not happening."

"You're hurt."

"Bruises will heal. The tenderness between my legs is because you're a big guy and, last I remember, we'd fucked like a dozen or so times." She paused, wanting to tease him into a better mood. "It was definitely fucking, but you licked me first and got me really wet. So, there was foreplay. It was pretty amazing too. You were rough but not brutal. I wasn't complaining. I was too busy getting off over and over. You're a stud."

"I don't know what that is."

"A machine. Sex, that is."

He closed his eyes and touched her forehead with his. He just stayed here, breathing her in, and she snuggled closer to his body. He eventually straightened up but pulled her into his arms, putting her on his lap. She liked it when he wrapped his arms around her.

"I'm fine, Cathian. Better than. Are you mad?"

"No." He pressed a kiss to the top of her head. "Surprised. Stunned that you did all that for me." He went quiet but then spoke again. "Relieved."

She rested her cheek against his chest, listening to his heart. "I wasn't going to lose you. I'd like to stay with you for as long as you'll let me."

"What about your shuttle? Your crew?"

"Truth?"

"Always between us."

"They can have my shuttle, for all I care. As I was flying away, I realized none of that mattered. I just wanted to return to you."

He hugged her tight. "I had my own regrets after you left."

She lifted her head to peer up at him. "Really?"

"I was afraid I'd kill you, Nara. But I didn't want anyone else. I swear I'm addicted to you."

That made her happy. "I hope you really are. It means you won't want me to leave or kick me off your ship again."

He unwrapped one arm and reached down, cupping her belly. "You could be carrying my litter." He looked worried.

"Would that upset you?"

"I'm more concerned about you, and how *you* feel about that."

"I knew I could get pregnant. See me here, still with you? I do have one demand though if I'm having your babies."

His body tensed beneath her. "What?"

"I don't want to leave *The Vorge* to go live on your home world, unless you're absolutely set on it. You didn't exactly sell me on the idea of the place after telling me how cold your people are and what life is like there. I'll go wherever you are, but that's my preference. Your crew loves you too, and they wouldn't want to lose you."

He cocked his head, staring at her. "How do you know that?"

She shrugged, breaking eye contact. "Just a feeling."

He released her stomach and cupped her face again, making her look up. She smiled.

His eyes narrowed—and then he surprised her by laughing. "They helped you, didn't they?"

"I *did* grab that stun gun from Dovis. He didn't give it to me, and he sure didn't want me to shoot him. He's probably pissed. You won't let him snarl at me or anything, will you?"

His humor faded. "He wouldn't dare."

"Good, because he dropped so hard onto the deck that I'm *still* flinching. I'm not the only one with bruises." She bit her lip. "I feel bad about that."

"You said you shot York too?"

"Yeah. He lay down before I stunned him, so he's fine. I needed access into your room. It wouldn't open for me."

"Of course." He chuckled again. "And Marrow? Did she let you choke her?"

Nara shook her head. "That would be a 'hell no.' I really choked her out and tied her up. Then we negotiated when she woke...but don't be mad."

"Tell me everything. I'm not angry. My crew always looks out for me. They had to know what my people did in the cargo hold, or quickly figured it out. They're under contract with the Tryleskian government, and interfering would have been grounds to terminate their employment and even face criminal charges."

"What exactly happened in the cargo hold?"

"You tell me everything first, and then I'll tell you what happened after you left."

She started from the moment she'd bucked into the shuttle and stopped when she shared her last memory of them on the bathroom floor. He took it all well.

She couldn't say the same for herself when she heard what Rex had done at the request of Cathian's father.

"Those assholes!" She wanted to beat some cat-men asses. "How could your own father do that to you? He was basically—"

"Calm down." He stroked her back. "Slow your breathing. You're panting."

"I'm pissed! I'm glad I shot that bitch in the ass. They were going to trap you in a loveless marriage by leaving you with no choice after knocking her up."

"You forgot to mention that part." He chuckled again. "You stunned her in the *ass*?"

"Well, I said I shot her. Sorry I left out the 'where.' I wasn't going to let her have you. You're mine."

His hand stilled on her back and his eyebrows rose.

"I went to a hell of a lot of trouble to defy you and get back on *The Vorge*. I was willing to battle your crew to be the one to get your seed, instead of some random woman. That sounds bad when I say it out loud, but there it is. If anyone was going to risk getting pregnant by you, it was going to be *me*. I took you on when you were all growly and snarly at me. That's love, Cathian. You couldn't even talk, and you were crawling instead of walking. You're seriously hot and definitely sexy, but kind of terrifying in the late stages of heat, baby. Do you think I'd have done all of that if I wasn't willing to do whatever it took to be with you?"

"You love me?"

She didn't look away from him. "Do you have a problem with that?"

"No. I do not. I *am* addicted to you." His hand lowered to gently caress her stomach. "My last thought before I blacked, out after being drugged, was wishing you were the one I could put my litter inside."

She could *already* be pregnant. Her heart raced. "I bet they would be adorable. How long before we know?"

"We could go have you scanned now."

"Let's do that in a little bit. Right now, I just want to stay in bed. Hey—I just noticed something. We're clean. Did we shower and forget? That's some drug you make."

"It's normal for the caregivers to bathe us while we're unconscious."

"Caregivers?"

"They came with Rex and the females. They would have bathed us both, cleaned up anything they needed to, put me in bed, and taken the female away." He frowned. "Shit. Rex will have been informed of what took place here."

"I'm not really caring if that dickhead is upset I knocked out that woman to be with you instead. I'm more concerned that people I don't know were touching me. That's creepy."

"I don't care about Rex's reaction either, but I'm curious why he allowed them to put you in bed with me." He stroked her once more. "The caregivers consist of older women. No males."

"I'm still creeped out. So little old ladies were washing you?" She didn't like that idea at all.

The door buzzed. Cathian lifted her off him and got out of bed. "Cover up," he ordered, rushing to put on some pants. She yanked up the covers but stayed seated upright. He went to the door and opened it.

"I had the Pods monitoring you both for when you awoke. Hungry? I figured you both would be. You've been sleeping for over twenty hours. Almost twenty-one. I was starting to worry."

"Come in." Cathian moved to the side.

The big blue alien walked in carrying a huge tray. He glanced at Nara and winked, before turning his attention to Cathian. "Where do you want it, Cap?"

"My desk. Is the Tryleskian shuttle still docked with us?"

"That would be a no." York placed the tray on the desk and faced his captain. "It's also why I'm the one delivering your food. Dovis is on the bridge, in case we're attacked."

Cathian was stunned. "What?"

"Shit got ugly," York admitted. He gave a slight nod of his head toward Nara and widened his eyes. "A certain assistant wanted to make an arrest. We figured you wouldn't like that."

His temper exploded. "Rex wanted to arrest Nara? For what?"

He heard her gasp but kept his full attention on York.

"Rex was informed by the wrinkled nags that they came in and found one furious unfucked female, who had been stunned in the butt by the woman you were curled around on the bathroom floor. Even in your sleep, you put up a fight when they tried to take her away from you." York's coloring darkened. "Are you sure you want to hear this?"

"Yes. Tell me all of it."

"Fuck. I was afraid you'd say that." York sighed. "The wrinkled nags couldn't get Nara away from you. You knocked some of them on their asses."

"Why are you calling them that? The caregivers consist of elders."

"'Elders' implies worthy of respect. Those women were yelling and bitching more than Marrow does when she's in the foulest mood. They were not happy, and you should see their faces when they are upset." He made a face, scrunching it up to mimic their expression. "Tons of wrinkles. I had to come in and separate you from her, Captain, to get you on the bed." He flashed a grin at Nara. "I didn't look. Not one bit."

That infuriated Cathian. York must have seen her naked. He snarled.

York snapped his head to him and took a step back, bumping into the desk. "I didn't look! Really. It was damn clear she's yours. You had a death grip on her. I was too busy wrestling you flat so the wrinkled nags could pull her clear of you. Don't get me started on the shower I had to take. I had your fluids all over me! I scrubbed for an hour and threw that damn uniform away. I still feel dirty, sir. I love you like a brother, but I *never* want to get that close to you again when you're naked."

"Fuck."

"You did. A lot." York had the nerve to chuckle. "The good news is, once I got you pinned and you weren't touching her anymore, you stopped fighting and began to snore. That's when one of the wrinkled nags called Rex. He ordered them to wash Nara and bring her to the shuttle. Said she was under arrest. I stepped out, called Dovis, but the Pods had already alerted him."

Cathian closed his eyes, mentally shouting to the Pods. He knew they'd hear him if he directed his thoughts at them. He opened his eyes and stormed to the door. He opened it and waited.

It didn't take long. The three of them came at him as fast as their short legs would allow. He stared at One.

"You—talk. Out loud. Nara needs to hear this."

"Yes, sir." One hesitated. "Rex was furious that the human ruined your father's plans to make you impregnate a Tryleskian. He feared he'd be fired, and decided the only way to redeem his honor was to bring the human back to be imprisoned, and give your father someone on whom to take out his anger." One paused. "He did not think about Nara possibly carrying your litter. He was too panicked about losing his job and status."

"What happened next?"

"We contacted Dovis to let him know, and he rushed to your cabin. He allowed York to go shower, since he was freaked out about having your sperm smeared all over him, worried that anyone would think you'd tried to hump him."

"Damn it, One," York yelled. "Stay out of my head. Rude!"

One rolled his eyes. "You did not try to hump him, Captain. Don't worry that you may have. You were in protective mode of your life-lock when they tried to take her from your arms. Your only thoughts were to keep her with you, to assure yourself she was safe. Part of you recognized York's scent during the struggle, and your instincts are to trust him. That's why you finally let her go. You understood she was safe with him. Then you went into a deeper sleep state. It's harder for us to pick up thoughts from there. They were too murky."

Cathian glanced at Nara. She remained on the bed with the covers around her body, but her gaze met his. It didn't appear as if she was alarmed.

He flushed, staring back at the Pods. *What next? And please don't mention again that I consider Nara my life-lock. We haven't talked about that yet.*

"Apologies," One whispered. "Dovis refused to allow the caregivers to take her. He escorted them back to their shuttle once you were both bathed. He personally carried her to your bed and placed her next to you. He thought you'd want her there." One paused and smiled. "He was right.

"Rex was enraged and frightened when he realized Dovis wouldn't give her up. He plans to return to Tryleskian and ask your father for a military transport, in order to return to us and take her by force. We warned Dovis. So he is on the bridge, ready to flee or battle with them, depending on how many transports they send, until you wake to give him orders. We informed him when you woke, and he's expecting you to call once you've been updated on the situation and fed. You're starving, and worried that Nara also needs food to recover."

"She is achy and sore, but thinks the sex and being with you were both worth it," Two whispered softly, making sure his voice didn't carry to the bed. "She loves you and is terrified you'll send her away again. She wants to stay with you and have your babies."

Three murmured, "Lots of babies that look like you, because they would be adorable." He paused. "Now she's wondering how long it will take her to heal because she wants to have sex with you again."

"That's enough," Cathian chuckled. He felt happy though. Nara wanted him and his litters. He was going to make that happen. "I'm going to eat with her. Inform Dovis—"

"We know." One turned away. "Just think it, and we'll tell him."

He backed into his room and nodded at York. "Thanks. You can go now."

His friend and crew member grinned. "I'm going." He paused as he passed. "I like her. She's a keeper."

"I know."

He sealed the door when he was alone with Nara. "Let's eat." He strode to the desk.

"Your people want to arrest me?"

He picked up the tray, carrying it to the bed. "It will be fine." He placed it down near her. "Don't be frightened."

She still looked at him with fear in her eyes. "Can they do that? I did break the law."

He shook his head. "I won't allow it. No one is taking you from me."

"Can you do that? Does your ambassador ranking overrule this Rex guy's authority?"

"Do you remember how you said I'm yours?"

She nodded.

"You're mine too, Nara. *No one* will take you from me. I'll handle my father and Rex."

She nodded but still looked concerned.

"Trust me."

Her gaze held his. "I do."

He pulled the lid off a place, his stomach rumbling from hunger at the scent of food. Midgel had prepared them a feast.

He grinned, silently sending a message to the Pods to give her his thanks.

He also told them to have Dovis notify him immediately if any military transports showed on the sensors.

Chapter Nine

Cathian stood on the bridge in front of the screen displaying his father. Rex stood next to Beltsen Vellar. Both Tryleskians were furious.

He understood—and felt the same way. "You will not arrest Nara."

"She assaulted Vis. A female from the Nooton House."

He inwardly flinched. That family had some power, but not nearly enough to compare to the Vellars. "Nara could be carrying my litter. Did either of you consider that?"

His father paled. "She's human!" He curled his lip in disgust. "That isn't acceptable. You are my firstborn, Cathian."

"The choice is mine. Not yours. Who I breed with won't be decided by *you*."

"We demand the human!" Rex replied.

Cathian glared at him. "You're an assistant. Heed your place. This is a discussion between my father and me."

Rex's face flushed and he dropped his gaze.

It was a dick move, but Cathian didn't care. Sometimes Rex overstepped his boundaries, and considering the man had tried to steal Nara away by arresting her, Cathian wasn't feeling any guilt.

He gave his full attention to his father. "Nara is mine."

"Cathian..." His father sat hard in the captain's chair of the military vessel he was currently on. "What are you saying?"

"I love her. She loves me."

His father snarled. "Love is a myth for fools."

"Are *you* happy, Father? Because I am." Cathian sighed, letting his temper go. "Do you know how I spent my morning, Father?"

His father glared at him.

"Laughing and playing with my Nara. We enjoy spending time together. She's still sore from getting me through my heat, and I'm unable to have sex with her for a few days. But it doesn't matter. It was a wonderful morning for us both because we were together. I've invited her to stay on *The Vorge* with me. It's done."

Beltsen Vellar growled. "But you're my firstborn. Your litters will be tainted by her human blood!"

Cathian's anger returned. "You have plenty of sons who will breed with Tryleskian females. And I'm the ambassador for our planet. Have you considered that? What better way to convince other races I'm trustworthy and open to their cultures than to life-lock to an alien woman and breed with her?"

His father seemed to consider that for long moments. He finally grinned. "That's why you want to keep her? I'm impressed."

"Don't be. I love Nara. That was my *only* motivation. But I knew you'd see the appeal of that argument."

That didn't make his father happy. "You're not returning to our planet with her?"

"No, Father. Part of the trust issues we've always had are due to switching ambassadors every few years, and the bonds we've formed with other races have to start anew. I plan to remain on *The Vorge* for a very long time."

"You can't raise children on a vessel."

"Lots of races do it."

"Not us!"

"It's time for change."

His father sighed and shook his head. "You were always difficult, never acting the way you should."

Cathian tensed, fearing another lecture on how he was such a disappointment. It wasn't something he enjoyed but it happened occasionally.

Beltsen stood, holding his gaze. "What if I continue to track *The Vorge* and take the female by force? She *did* break the law when she shot Vis and interfered with your heat. I'm sure I could persuade the medical staff to end any pregnancy under those circumstances. Don't let this be about pride, son. I understand the protective instincts in regards to your young, but humans are a weak race. Think of the possible flaws in those children."

Cathian's hands fisted, and he wanted to hit his father. "Try to take her. I'll use every weapon on this ship to stop you."

"You'd *threaten* me?"

"Nara is my life-lock."

His father gasped, eyes wide. "NO!"

"What do you think I've been telling you by explaining that I love her? That she's staying with me and probably carrying my litter?"

"She's human! You can't life-lock to one. It might not even be possible!"

"The bond is there. I feel it. That's all that matters."

"Does *she*?" Rex leaned close to the screen.

Cathian wanted to ignore him but knew his father would just repeat the question. "I believe so. She went to extreme effort to be with me during my heat, despite knowing it risked her life."

His father sagged back into the chair. "Only you, Cathian. Always so rebellious."

"You'll leave Nara alone. It's not up for debate. She's *mine*."

His father waved his hand. "Fine. Perhaps this will be a good thing. I've viewed footage of humans. They are pathetic…seeing one on your arm while you take meetings will show others we have compassion."

Cathian bit back a snarl.

"Hopefully they won't view *us* as pathetic." His father's eyes narrowed suddenly. "What if they do, Cathian? Think that because you're life-locked to something so weak, our planet is ripe for war?" He shook his head. "We can't risk that. I'm ordering you home with this female. Dax is onboard with me. He'll take over."

Cathian filled with fury. "No!"

Dovis suddenly stormed up next to him. He glanced at his friend, surprised that he'd interrupt instead of staying out of view.

Dovis snarled, showing his fangs. "He has *me* at his side. No one would be that stupid. The Pods can also read minds. If anyone thinks such a thing, I'll be happy to show them the error of their ways."

Beltsen scoffed. "You? You'll snarl at them and show them your teeth? How is that supposed to frighten anyone?"

Dovis shook his head. "Not just me. York is a Parri. Any race that is a threat, the Pods will warn us. We're a fierce crew—and Raff is onboard too."

Both men on the screen paled.

Cathian knew the reason why. So did Dovis. His friend spoke to Beltsen again before he could.

"Your brother abandoned his firstborn son to a planet of *thieves and mutants*, as you call them. Raff survived by learning how to kill anyone who became a threat. And he was so good at it, the Gluttren Four government made him their number one assassin. His body count is near legendary."

Beltsen paled. "We do not speak of such things."

Cathian jumped on that opportunity. "I will—if you forced me to quit and return home with Nara."

"You wouldn't dare." Rex broke out in a sweat. "You'd harm the Vellar name!"

"I don't care," Cathian stated, meaning his words. He glared at his father. "You covered it up. When your brother got a female pregnant, instead of life-locking to her, he abandoned her on that hellhole of a planet. I went and found Raff. He's a part of my crew now. Do you think if I'm forced to come home, he might return with me?"

His *father* broke into a sweat now.

Cathian had to resist flat-out grinning. Dovis was a genius to bring up Raff. It was exactly the bargaining chip they needed. "Never threaten Nara, Father. Never force me to return to our planet. I'm doing an excellent job representing our race. No one will see us as weak with the crew I've acquired. Having a human on my arm will only make other races envious of her beauty, and think we're capable of compassion. It's never a bad thing."

"You're threatening *me*." His father shook his head, looking angry now. "How dare you?"

"You threaten my life-lock. My future and happiness. I won't stand for it." Cathian glared at him. "Understood?"

The two men on screen consulted each other, whispering.

Dovis leaned in closer and snorted. Cathian met his gaze, grateful that they were friends. The crew stuck together. They were a family, always having each other's backs.

The whispering stopped. Cathian turned back to Beltsen. "I'm keeping Nara, Father. I'll defend her with my life. You can either continue to meet *The Vorge*, and start the biggest scandal in our planet's history, or congratulate me."

Rex whispered furiously in his father's ear.

"Fine, Cathian. I won't have everyone talking about how our ambassador used our own ship to fire on our military. I think you've lost your mind though."

"No. You fear the Vellar name will be tarnished by what you and your brother once did, more than anything else. And I haven't lost my mind, I just refuse to be miserable the way you are. Any children I have with Nara will know happiness. They won't grow up watching us playing cruel games with each other."

His father glared but gave a sharp nod. "I hope you're right. We'll return to our planet." He paused. "I *do* plan to send Dax to your ship at some point. Not to take over your job, but to get him out of my hair. He's as annoying as you were at that age."

Cathian grinned. "That's fine. I'll find something for him to do."

The screen went blank. Dovis marched across the room, bent to check a monitor, and seconds passed before he said, "They're turning around and changing course."

"That went better than I thought it would. Thank you for reminding me that we had the upper hand."

Dovis straightened and faced him. "Your father *did* have a point. Your children could turn out more human. Are you prepared for that?"

"I remember when you were poisoned on that backward planet we visited, and you couldn't keep your fur on." It had shocked him when he'd first seen Dovis shift into another form, one with skin. "I didn't think less of you. I felt honored that you trusted me to care for you when your defenses were down. Even then, without your claws and fangs, you were fierce. No one else survived the poison you were shot with. Pure willpower alone kept you alive until it was out of your system. Nara is stronger than you think, Dovis."

Dovis nodded. "She stole my stunner. Her *reflexes* are definitely faster than I estimated."

"She took me on when I was mindless in my heat, knowing I could kill her. She's very brave."

"I'll try to like her."

Cathian grinned. "Good. She's staying."

"Do you think she can carry your litters safely?"

That quickly killed his good mood. "I hope so. I've read a lot about humans. Sometimes they carry twins and triplets. I've ordered our medical android to download every program available on her race. I'm taking her for an exam now. I wanted to deal with my father first."

"Do you want her to be pregnant?"

"I'd be thrilled."

"I thought you didn't want to have children yet." Dovis frowned.

"I didn't, but things change. I hadn't met Nara yet."

"I've got the bridge. Go be with her."

"Thanks again."

Nara was nervous as Cathian took her into their medical facility on *The Vorge*. An android waited. It was white, with four limbs shaped like those of a humanoid.

A table lifted from the floor and she climbed on it, as instructed.

"Scanning the female from Earth now," the android stated.

"Did you upload everything you could find on her race?" Cathian stayed close to her.

"Affirmative." The android paused. "She is not carrying your young. There's an implant."

Nara was stunned. "I don't have an implant."

A holo-image appeared over her stomach, displaying her insides, along with a foreign object.

"It has been registered to the Orits."

Cathian sighed.

"Who? What?" Nara was confused.

"The auction house is owned by them. They must have implanted you before the sale to prevent you from getting pregnant."

That upset her. Not only was she disappointed not to be pregnant, but those alien asshats had done something to her body without telling her! She blinked back tears. "I'm sorry. I didn't know."

Cathian smiled at her and gently put his hand on her shoulder. "It's fine. In three years, we'll be better ready to become parents. This will give us some alone time. Maybe it's for the best."

"You're disappointed."

"A little, but it's a good thing, Nara. I like the idea of having a few years with just you."

She couldn't argue that.

Cathian turned to the android. "Can you safely remove the implant?"

"Yes."

He looked back at her. "I can't get you pregnant until my next heat. Do you want the implant removed?"

"Yes." She wanted it out. Some foreign object had been installed in her uterus without her permission. For all she knew it could have a tracking device on it, or something worse.

"Do it," Cathian ordered. "I'm right here."

The android gave her a shot, and in seconds, she passed out.

When she came around, Cathian was there, still with his hand on her shoulder.

She reached down, exploring her stomach with her fingers. She didn't feel any bandages.

"It didn't have to cut it out?"

"It did but the wound has sealed and healed."

She sat up, looking at her belly. "I don't see anything."

"You won't. We have good medical technology. The implant has been removed."

She looked at the android in the corner. "Thank you."

"My pleasure," it stated.

Cathian helped her off the table. "Let's go to our cabin."

"I feel great."

"The android gave you something to progress your healing. Your planet is generous with their information sharing. He had access to all their records on all medical procedures and human biology. He can treat you for anything now."

They reached his cabin, and Cathian ushered her in first. She came to stop when she saw what waited. Someone had come in since they'd left and laid out a feast on their bed.

She turned, looking at him.

Cathian grinned. "Romantic?"

"Very. Thank you." She blinked back tears. "This was to celebrate my pregnancy though, wasn't it? I'm so sorry."

"I called York while you were being operated on to bring us food. Don't apologize again for that, Nara. Never. The more I think of it, I'm glad we get to wait three years. Babies are a wonderful thing, but they put a strain on romance and bonding. Especially since there would be at least two to five of them. Caring for that many infants would tire us out." He smiled. "Now we can concentrate on each other. Not a bad thing."

She nodded. "I agree."

He took her hand and led her to the bed. She went to sit but he suddenly pulled her close, staring into her eyes. "Before we dig in, there's something I'd like to discuss with you."

"Okay."

He took a deep breath and lowered his head, his face inches from hers. "I'd like to life-lock to you. Would you agree to that?"

"Yes!" She didn't even have to think about it.

He smiled wide and hugged her. "Good."

"What do we need to do?"

"It's what you would consider a medical procedure."

"Okay."

He waited.

She just stared back at him. Finally, he frowned.

"Aren't you going to ask what kind? What is involved?"

"I don't care. I'm willing to do it. It doesn't matter."

He smiled again. "I love you."

"I love you too."

"Male Tryleskians have a secondary small heart in our chests. When we life-lock to a female, it is implanted in *her* chest. It links us by scent. The android feels it would be safe for humans. It's never been done before." He lifted his hand, curving his finger to his thumb, demonstrating a small round shape the size of a small coin. "It's about this size."

She let that information settle. "Okay."

"That doesn't frighten you?"

"No. I was willing to have your litters. What's a tiny piece of you inside my body?" She smiled. "I like that. I'll be the keeper of your other heart. That's romantic."

He chuckled. "Humans are strange but I'm grateful."

"You should have asked me while we were with the medical android. Can he do it for us now?"

"Tomorrow. Now, we eat and celebrate. We are to be life-locked. I'm glad you came into my life, Nara."

"Me too." She already couldn't imagine life without him.

Chapter Ten

Nara took a seat on the bridge, mindful of Dovis watching her. He wasn't her biggest fan but they had a sort of truce going since Cathian was someone they both loved.

She reached up and touched her chest. The spot where Cathian's secondary heart had been transplanted was warmer to the touch than the skin around it, as if it were a mini radiator.

Two weeks had passed since they'd done the surgery. He'd worried about there being a chance of rejection, since they were two different races. It hadn't happened though.

The android had told her privately that it wasn't technically a heart but Tryleskians preferred that term. It was more like a small organ that produced a chemical to make her smell exactly like the male the female had received it from. Dobs—what she'd named the android—had tested her many times. It was working correctly. Her body produced the scent that assured Cathian she belonged to him, thus locking them together. She was the only woman he'd want and be drawn to. She'd effectively become an extension of Cathian.

She checked her messages again, hoping this time there would be a response.

One showed—and her heart pounded as she tapped on the video message.

Belinda's face came into view, and she smiled. "Hey! We got your message. Derrick is with me."

He leaned into view and gave her a goofy grin. "You fell in love with the dick that bought you, huh? Not surprised. That happens when you never get laid."

Belinda elbowed him hard in the gut and he jerked away, out of sight. "Ignore him. We're happy for you. Really. And no worries. When I got to the shuttle, Derrick was already there with the part. He even installed it without bitching and moaning. We're at Rogerville right now. We came hoping to find you, since we had to fly out of the storage yard. We didn't want to get caught stealing the shuttle; they've increased patrols. Imagine our surprise when we had a message waiting here from you."

Derrick leaned back into view. "I can't believe you're giving us your baby. That's so cool of you."

Belinda nodded. "Fifty-fifty owners. Thank you, Nara." She teared up. "You know if it doesn't work out with your guy, though, that you're always our captain. We'll give it back."

"Hey!" Derrick scowled. "We'll give her a third. I've never owned a shuttle before. Don't be giving it all away when we just found out we have one."

Belinda rolled her eyes. "I'm stuck with him forever now. Couldn't you have made *me* owner and kept him my mechanic? That way I could fire him when he's annoying me to death."

"She loves me."

Belinda elbowed him again. "You wish. I put up with you because you're good at fixing shit. And Nara felt sorry for you, bonehead. Maybe she just thinks you'll get repairs done if you're half owner, instead of thinking with your dick."

Derrick hesitated. "Fair enough. And true."

Nara grinned.

Belinda lifted a hand and blew her a kiss. "We got a job hauling mining equipment to Cornel Moon. We leave in two hours. It's good money, and no one should want to shoot us for it."

"Besides the people we got away from. Some scary woman with bone jewelry bought me." He shuddered. "I told her I was shy and needed some alone time before she could ride my dick. I fled and stole a transport. She might be looking for me, so I don't want to stay in one place for long." He pointed at Belinda. "Her blue guy might be looking for her too, but of course she did him first before getting away. He might be in a mellower mood."

Belinda rolled her eyes. "As if anyone would want you enough to go to extreme lengths to try to find you. Bone-alien lady is probably relieved. She probably saw your little dick and had buyer's remorse."

"It's hardly little. Want me to show you?"

"No!"

Derrick looked bummed and stared at the screen, mouthing *she does want it*. "Sorry we couldn't wait around to talk to you for real, Nara," Derrick said aloud. "We need the money from this job. But leave us messages and we should be at a port soon. Thank you for the shuttle."

"Yeah. Thank you, Nara. Be happy." Belinda ended the message.

"Your friends are strange."

She turned her head, staring at Dovis. "I know."

"You gave them your shuttle? Why? You could have sold it."

"Trading is what they do for a living. They'd have had to find new jobs, and trust me, it's best if they stick together. Humans aren't well liked by some races. I know those two will watch out for each other."

"The female wasn't full human."

"And she gets a lot of shit for it. Not from Derrick, though. I think he's secretly in love with her. He's always flirting. Now they can stay together."

"You could have earned a lot of money for the sale."

"Money doesn't matter. Knowing the two of them have a secure future does."

Dovis stared at her and finally nodded. "You are a good person."

She stood up. "Thanks, Dovis. I'm going to hunt down Cathian."

"He's exercising."

She left the bridge and found the gym. The sight of Cathian hanging from bars on the ceiling and doing pull-ups instantly made her girl parts warm. He was beautiful and she loved seeing all those muscles bulging and flexing with every move.

He saw her and dropped to the floor. A big grin spread across his lips. "My Nara."

"I heard from my crew. They got the shuttle, and even have their first job."

He grabbed hold of her in a bear hug, lifting her from her feet. "I knew it would turn out well. You've been too worried."

She wrapped her arms around his shoulders and planted a kiss on his lips. "I'm just glad they were able to escape, and the shuttle was still there for them to take."

"Me too. I would have routed us that way, but we have to prove to my father that I can still do this job with you at my side. I have Glaxions to impress and open trade negotiations with. He's looking for any reason to make Dax as my replacement."

Guilt surfaced. "I'm sorry."

"It's not your fault."

"I feel as if it is."

"It's not, Nara. My father is a shaft-head."

She chuckled. "You mean a dickhead?"

He nodded. "Same thing. I don't care what he thinks as long as he leaves us alone. He will. I'll get the Glaxions signed, and then after a few station stops, we'll visit the Teki station in about ten months for our annual repairs and upgrades on *The Vorge*." He paused. "I plan to have them do a little remodeling while we're there."

"What kind?"

He hesitated. "There are some empty visitors' quarters behind mine. I thought I'd add two of them to our cabin for when I go into heat next time. We'll have bedrooms for our children."

She was touched. "That's a few years from now."

"I like to plan things in advance, and that way, the space is already allotted to us in case my father does send my brother—or brothers—to *The Vorge*. It's also better we have them remodeled now than while you're pregnant. It's a nice station for having repairs done. They have a lot of entertainment venues to amuse crews stuck there during repairs. I thought it would make for a nice honeymoon. I apologize it's such a long wait."

"Don't be. That's so sweet."

"I told you I did my research on humans." He grinned. "I also sent a message to Earth."

She was surprised. "You did? Why? Are you planning to open trade negotiations with them?"

"No. I have the only thing I want from that planet right here in my arms. I sent a message to your ex-husband."

Stunned, she gaped at him. "Why?"

"To tell him you belong to *me* now, and that he'd better never dare think about harassing you again. I flashed teeth and snarled a lot. I imagine he pissed his pants if he's intelligent."

She laughed, picturing her ex's reaction to an angry Cathian staking his claim. "I love you."

"You aren't mad?"

"No. I wish I could have seen his face though. He probably *did* wet his pants."

"I wanted to make sure he knew you were off-limits and I'd defend you with my life."

"Thank you."

The doors opened and Marrow came in. "Geez. Not again. You two are always kissing and touching. Give it a rest. Some of us come in here to exercise."

Cathian lowered Nara and put her down. "We're leaving. The space is all yours." He took her hand. "Nara and I will be in our cabin."

Marrow snorted. "Of course you will. You're making me want a mate."

The doors opened again and York came in. "Who wants to spar?"

"Nobody," Marrow muttered. "Those two are about to go have sex. I came to work up a sweat."

"Sex sweat?" York rubbed his hands together. "I can help you with that."

Cathian walked toward the door, taking Nara with him. "I don't want to know if you two are doing the wild thing, but take it to one of your cabins. Dovis gets pissed if you use one of the general areas. He's due for rounds soon. You don't want him to catch you bare."

They returned to their cabin, and Cathian drew a bath. Nara loved taking one with him. He settled into the warm water first, and she climbed in and leaned against his chest. "This is so nice."

"It is."

"This is the life."

He chuckled. "True. My crew is even happy. I'm not spending my time looking over their shoulders. Instead, I'm relaxing in baths with you."

"I have no complaints if you want to look over my shoulder."

He leaned forward a little, staring down. "I love your breasts."

She chuckled. "I love when you touch them."

He slid his hands up her body. "Me too."

Epilogue

A hand rubbed Nara's ass, a big warm one, and a firm male body rested against her back. She turned her head to peer at Cathian curled around her back, his hand propping his head up. His sexy golden gaze met hers.

"How are you?"

She grinned. "Today is the day, isn't it?"

"We've reached the Teki station and have two weeks of lavish hotel accommodations and entertainment. Our honeymoon begins."

She couldn't wait. The last ten months had been busy. First, they'd gone to see the Glaxions. They were a race that reminded her of dog people, almost like Dovis, but they made him seem friendly. That was saying a lot, since Cathian's best friend could be grumpy and growly. Her life-lock had won them over though, and opened trade negotiators for his planet.

It seemed Glaxions were incredibly advanced in medical technology. To prove how much, they'd offered to run some tests on Nara and Cathian. She'd been leery, but he'd encouraged it, since they were known as the leading experts when it came to breeding with other races.

The doctor had assured that when Cathian went into heat, Nara shouldn't have any problems getting pregnant, now that the implant was long gone. They'd even established that she'd have two to three babies, instead of five; that her pregnancy would last five months instead of nine; and their infants should be born at around six pounds each.

Cathian had sent that information to his father, to prove it was possible for him to breed with her. She knew his father gave him headaches about that, since she hadn't conceived during the first heat. The testing alone was worth getting him off her life-lock's ass. He had enough stress to deal with being an ambassador.

After that, they'd traveled to at least five stations for what Cathian called "boring meetings" to keep his relationships steady with other races. She'd stayed aboard *The Vorge* for most of them, since they were on pretty rough stations. Dovis had claimed she was a high-priority target to slavers, safer onboard. She was fine with that.

Now they could finally relax for a couple weeks.

They showered, grabbed their bags, and met the rest of the crew near the airlock to the station. Everyone looked excited except Dovis. He was there without a bag.

Cathian scowled. "Every member of the crew gets a two-week vacation. That includes you."

"No. One of us needs to remain onboard and protect this vessel from theft." Dovis crossed his arms over his hairy chest. "I don't want or need a vacation."

He spat that last word like it was an insult.

Nara watched both men, identifying the signs of an upcoming fight. She still didn't know Dovis well but, over the months, she'd learned that he wasn't a social creature. "Baby, if he wants to stay, let him."

Cathian growled. "He needs to take time off."

"He'll be alone. That's probably restful for him," she pointed out, and then lowered her voice. "He doesn't seem to like people. This probably *is* his version of vacation."

York laughed. "Nara's got a point there, Cap. We're all leaving. Dovis is happier than shit."

"Fine," Cathian sighed. "Don't terrorize the repair crews. No snarling, no watching them while they work and making them so nervous they flee. You already scared off our engineer, making Harver quit three months ago."

Nara hid a grin. She could see that Dovis looked disappointed with that order, but he gave a sharp nod.

Cathian put his arm around her. "Ready for some fun, life-lock?"

"Sure am!" She waved at Dovis. "Enjoy the peace and quiet."

"I will."

They left the ship and entered the station. It was massive for a repair place. The Teki were known for owning a chain of them. It was busy when they reached one of the main arteries of the station, various alien races strolling by.

"Cross your fingers for me. I'm searching for a mate," Marrow whispered. "See you around the station."

"Two weeks," Cathian reminded her. "Don't make me hunt you down."

York frowned. "I thought maybe we could spend the time together, Marrow."

She glanced at him. "Sorry. You're a great lover, York. It's just that we wouldn't make good mates." She stalked off without another word.

York watched her go and sighed.

Cathian reached over and squeezed his arm. "Easy, big guy. There are lots of females on the station."

Midgel cleared her throat lightly. "You could be my escort, York. I'm afraid to go anywhere by myself."

York was definitely the protective type. "Okay. Let's go, Midgel. I'll keep you safe."

The Pods stood with the last silent member of their crew. The Tryleskian male never spoke. One did all the talking for him. "Raff wants to watch shows with us. We'll be fine, Captain. He's scary enough that no one will mess with us."

Nara glanced at Raff. She wasn't sure what he did on *The Vorge*, rarely saw him actually, and Cathian avoided answering questions about him. He was young and handsome. All she knew for sure was that he was a Vellar, a cousin or some other distant relative of Cathian's.

"Have fun."

That left Nara and Cathian alone. He grinned down at her. "It's just us. You ready to check into that nice hotel suite I told you about? I went with a jungle theme."

"I can't wait."

"You, me, and a bed in a tree."

She laughed. "Sounds fun, unless I fall out and it's a big drop."

His arm around her tightened. "I'd never allow you to get hurt."

She believed that. "Let the honeymoon begin."

He led her to the left, where there was a sign with the universal symbol for accommodations. "It also has a waterfall shower."

"Even better."

"Only the best for you."

They got checked in at the desk and took a lift up to the room. Cathian unlocked the door and threw it open, dropping their bags, then he picked her up and carried her inside. She stared at the big indoor space. It really was themed like some star-filled night in a jungle, with lots of trees, and four moons displayed across the ceiling.

"This is fantastic."

"This is what my planet looks like outside of the cities. I don't ever want to return there to live, but I wanted you to see it. They did a pretty realistic job. It's like an upgraded version of camping, since we have a bathroom, room service, and a real bed up in that tree over there."

"It's beautiful."

He peered down at her and smiled. "*You're* beautiful. And mine. My sweet Nara, the keeper of my heart." His golden gaze narrowed with passion.

She liked that. "And my Captain Cathian, the keeper of *my* heart."

"We're going to be very happy."

She knew they would be. Some lucky people met their soul mates…and she'd found hers. "I already am."

"Me too."

Not the end. Up next, Dovis.

About the Author

NY Times and USA Today Bestselling Author

I'm a full-time wife, mother, and author. I've been lucky enough to have spent over two decades with the love of my life and look forward to many, many more years with Mr. Laurann. I'm addicted to iced coffee, the occasional candy bar (or two), and trying to get at least five hours of sleep at night.

I love to write all kinds of stories. I think the best part about writing is the fact that real life is always uncertain, always tossing things at us that we have no control over, but when writing you can make sure there's always a happy ending. I love that about being an author. My favorite part is when I sit down at my computer desk, put on my headphones to listen to loud music to block out everything around me, so I can create worlds in front of me.

For the most up to date information, please visit my website. www.LaurannDohner.com

Printed in Great Britain
by Amazon